NINE LIVES

JORDAN QUEST FBI THRILLER SERIES, BOOK 4

Gary Winston Brown

GARY WINSTON BROWN

NINE LIVES

JORDAN QUEST SERIES BOOK 4

COPYRIGHT & AUTHOR'S NOTE

COPYRIGHT

AUTHOR'S NOTE

This is a work of fiction. Names, characters, places and incidents – and their usage for storytelling purposes – are crafted for the singular purpose of fictional entertainment and no absolute truths shall be derived from the information contained within. Locales, businesses, companies, events, government institutions, law enforcement agencies and private institutions are used for atmospheric, entertainment and fictional purposes only. Furthermore, any resemblance or reference to persons living or dead is used fictitiously for atmospheric, entertainment and fictional purposes.

"There's no chance, no destiny, no fate, that
can circumvent
or hinder or control the firm resolve
of a determined soul."

Ella Wheeler

For my beautiful wife,
Fiona.

ILYBBOBKS

PROLOGUE

SARASOTA, FLORIDA

The teens stared in disbelief at the words on the computer screen: DOWNLOAD COMPLETE.

The cursor blinked, awaited their next command.

"Whoa, Tommy," Billy Reynolds said, his words tinged with elements of both excitement and fear. "Do you realize what you just did?"

Tommy Moore sat back in his chair and let out a long sigh. "Yeah," he replied. "I just hacked the goddamn Department of Defense."

The logo for the Defense Advanced Research Projects Agency stared back at them from the screen.

"DARPA is supposed to be unhackable," Billy said. "How the hell did you do it?"

Tommy smiled. "I'm a frickin' genius," he replied.

Billy stood, paced around his friend's bedroom. He was nervous, scared. He rubbed his hands together, wiped his face. "Jesus Christ, Tommy," he said. "This is no ordinary hack. This is way over the line. If they find out you got in…"

"They won't."

1

"But if they do..."

"Nothing will happen. Trust me."

"Easy for you to say," Billy exclaimed. "But when the military busts into your parents' house in the middle of the night..."

"This computer will be gone," Tommy said. He removed the USB drive onto which he had saved the files from the machine. The first file was named CHANNELER, the second LEEDA. He put the drive in his pocket. "Besides, it's their own damn fault. This division, Dynamic Life Sciences, must be a small-time operation. Their whole system crashed less than a minute after I got in. What kind of military operation would leave themselves that vulnerable?"

"Listen to me, Tommy," Billy warned. "You're in way over your head. You need to erase those files now. Do you even know the first thing about DARPA?"

"Should I care?"

"Damn right! They're the military's technological division. We're talking cutting-edge defensive shit... weapons, anti-terrorism, out-of-the-box science-fiction stuff... the likes of which you can't even imagine."

Tommy opened the file folder and hovered the cursor over the file that read CHANNELER.

"I'm warning you, man," Billy said. "Don't open it. Leave well enough alone. You hacked into DLS. Congratulations. You hit the big time. You're officially a fucking black hat legend. Now take my advice and fry that thing."

"I can't do that," Tommy said.

"Why the hell not?"

"I need to know what it is."

"What *what* is?"

"Project Channeler."

"I'm telling you, you're playing with fire. Open that file and you're dead."

"You worry too much, you know that?" Tommy said. He clicked on the file.

The computer display turned black. The words DEPARTMENT OF DEFENSE, EYES ONLY suddenly appeared on screen.

Billy grabbed his knapsack from the floor beside his chair. "That's it," he said. "I don't want to have anything to do with this."

"You never did," Tommy said. "This was my hack, not yours."

"You know what I mean," Billy snapped. "You have no idea how much shit you're in now, Tommy. This isn't a backdoor hack to get paid a few bucks for adjusting exam marks or wiping out somebody's credit card balance. This is a breach of national security. When DARPA figures out it's been compromised, which they will 'cause they're fucking *DARPA*, they're going to come after you with everything they've got. Your life as you know it will be over. We're talking lock-the-door-and-throw-away-the-key jail time, man." Billy pulled on his baseball cap and slung his backpack over his shoulder. "Good luck, Tommy," he said. "You're gonna need it. I'm outa here."

"Wimp," Tommy replied.

"Absolutely!" Billy said. "But at least I'll be a *free* wimp. Enjoy your time in prison, asshole."

"Whatever," Tommy replied. He paid no attention to his friend as he left his bedroom. He was completely mesmerized by the information on the screen. What was Project Channeler, and what made it so important as to have been given EYES ONLY security classification?

Tommy scrolled through the file which had been authored by Dr. Jason Merrick, the Director of the facility. The case notes were exhaustive and detailed the projects advancements. Tommy paged to the end of the file to the section that read CONCLUSIONS. He read the summation:

'Clinical trial and critical evaluation process an unprecedented success. Test subject, Commander Ben Egan, fully integrated. Neural download, DNA and biometric enhancement, sympathetic nervous system, metabolic, physical, psychic, extra-sensory and telekinetic capabilities have surpassed project expectations. Recommendation: Field trial continuance, covert assignment. If successful, candidate will be advanced to phase two, Life Extending Epidermal Defensive Augmentation, aka. LEEDA'.

Tommy's mouth dropped as he read the report.

Billy was right. He *was* in way over his head.

Terrified at the possibility of who or *what* might soon come looking for him, Tommy unplugged the laptop, ran downstairs, threw open the back door and hurried outside to his father's toolshed. He grabbed a can of gasoline from the corner, doused the computer in the noxious liquid, set it ablaze, then stepped back and watched the machine hiss, pop, crackle and burn.

After several minutes he extinguished the fire. The device had been destroyed.

Tommy knew his attempt to destroy the machine had done nothing to eliminate the trail of electronic breadcrumbs which might have been left by his hack.

With any luck, he had gotten in and out, sight unseen.

ARLINGTON, VIRGINIA

U.S. DEPARTMENT OF DEFENSE,
DEFENSE ADVANCED RESEARCH PROJECTS
AGENCY (DARPA)
OFFICE OF COLONEL QUENTIN HALLIER

Colonel Hallier reviewed the report of the incident which had occurred at Dynamic Life Sciences, DARPA's clandestine medical and military advancement laboratory. The detonation of an electromagnetic pulse bomb had utterly destroyed its data center less than forty-eight hours ago. According to the electronic file, the contents of which was being updated hourly, Dr. Jason Merrick had been responsible for the murder of several of his colleagues, after which he had set out with Commander Ben Egan, his field test subject for Project Channeler, on a spree of death and destruction which had culminated in the near destruction of the California State University at Long Beach and the taking of many civilian, police and military lives. He had taken the hit from his superiors for the mind-numbing catastrophic consequences of the attack, and rightly so. If there had been warning signs, he'd never seen them. Now Merrick was dead, and Egan's disappearance from the scene was classified, TOP SECRET. Hallier had reason to believe the commander might still be alive, although his whereabouts were unknown. Projects Channeler and LEEDA had gone off the rails, the technology stolen by Merrick and used to exact a matter of personal revenge. The hundreds of millions of dollars in research invested to create the world's foremost super soldier had also disappeared in the person of Commander Ben Egan. GENESIS had been terminated. Hallier was thankful he hadn't been terminated with it.

Alan Rober, the colonel's personal aide, knocked on his door.

"Enter," Hallier called out.

Rober waved a sheet of paper in his hand as he entered the office. "Sir, you need to see this," he said.

"See what?"

"The computer login report from Dynamic Life Sciences."

"What report? We lost everything in the breach, including the servers. We had no backups."

"That's correct, sir. But we still have the external access report."

"What are you talking about?" Hallier asked.

"The EMP destroyed the facility and all the computer files and equipment within it. But our security firewalls continued to log each and every keystroke and IP address leading up to the attack. Less than a minute before it destroyed the lab, we encountered a level three cyberattack."

"Meaning?"

"In layman's terms, we were hacked."

Hallier sat back in his chair. "How in God's name…"

Rober shook his head. "I don't know, sir. How they could get into the DLS network is beyond me, but they did."

"How bad was it?"

"As far as we can tell, two files were downloaded before the system went dark: Projects Channeler and LEEDA."

Hallier stood, snapped up the paper from his desk. "Are you telling me that someone out there has those files?"

Rober nodded. "That's the way it appears, sir."

"Do we know where to find them?"

"Possibly," the aide answered. "The hack was sophisticated, but we think it originated here in the States."

"Where?"

"A residential address. Sarasota, Florida."

Hallier picked up his phone and placed a call.

"Field Operations, Commander Leighton."

"Commander, this is Hallier. I need a high value target recovery team on the tarmac and ready to roll within the hour. The mission is top secret. I'll provide you with the details when I arrive."

"Copy that, sir. We'll be waiting for you."

Hallier hung up. "How much do we know about the threat?"

"Nothing, sir," Rober said. "Just a location based on a registered IP address."

Hallier opened his desk drawer, removed his sidearm, holstered the weapon and walked out of his office. "Get me to Field Ops," he said.

Rober followed closely behind. "Copy that, sir."

CHAPTER 1

SPECIAL AGENT CHRIS HANOVER pressed the intercom button and waited outside the gated entrance to the Quest family mansion.

To his left, the light on the security camera stand blinked from red to green. Chris looked into the lens and smiled. "Hey, Marissa," he said. "It's me. Is Jordan available?"

The housekeeper's pleasant voice replied. "Good morning, Agent Hanover. Yes, of course. Please drive in."

"Thanks," Chris replied.

The heavy gates slowly parted. Chris drove up the winding driveway and parked under the portico outside the front entrance. The front door opened as he walked up the steps. Emma and Aiden, Jordan's children, raced outside to meet him with Lucy, the children's Golden Retriever pup and newest addition to their family, hot on their heels. The dog barked playfully as the children rushed into his arms.

"Chris!" Aiden yelled.

Emma locked her arms around Chris' neck and gave him a giant hug.

"Hey, monsters," Chris said as he returned their affection. "Have you two been good for Marissa while your mom was away?"

"Always!" Aiden said.

"*Always?*" Chris joked. "I find that hard to believe."

Lucy joined in on the action. The pup gnawed and pulled on the agents pant leg, then rolled onto her back, having successfully negotiated her way into a vigorous belly rub.

Chris picked the children up in his arms as Lucy raced back inside. "How's Lucy doing?" he asked. "Is she settling in okay?"

Rescued by Jordan from the scene of a recent murder in Beverly Hills, the pup had been adopted just days before. Judging by her exuberant behavior and bond with the children, the decision had been a good one. Lucy appeared to be thriving in her new home.

"She sleeps on my pillow with her butt in my face," Aiden said.

"Gross!" Emma exclaimed.

"I'd rather have her butt in my face than your butt in my face," Aiden replied.

Marissa joined them in the vestibule. Chris put down the children and gave her a hug. "How are you, Marissa?" he asked.

"I'm well, Agent Hanover," Marissa replied. "Thank you for asking."

"Where's the lady of the house?" Chris asked, referring to Jordan.

"On the shooting range in the west wing. Shall I call her for you?"

"That's all right," Chris replied. "Mind if I wander through and find her?"

Marissa smiled. "Not at all. You know the way."

"Thanks, Marissa." To the twins he said, "Okay, you two. Hustle your buns inside. I need to talk to your mom. Cop stuff."

"Can we play later?" Aiden asked.

Chris smiled. "I think I can manage that," he said.

"Cool!" Aiden yelled.

Chris walked through the massive mansion until he reached the door to the Training Room. Inside, gunshots reverberated off the walls of the indoor firing range as Jordan discharged the weapon. He pressed the call buzzer on the wall. The firing suddenly stopped. Seconds later Jordan opened the door.

"Taking out your frustrations on poor defenseless targets?" Chris joked as he walked into the room.

Jordan smiled. "Just trying to stay sharp."

"That's never been your problem," Chris said. "I hope you don't mind me stopping by. I wanted to check up on the kids, see how they were doing."

"That was sweet of you," Jordan replied.

"Of course, it was. I'm the sweetest guy you'll ever know."

"Modest, too"

"Don't forget devilishly handsome."

"How could I? You're always reminding me."

"True." Chris said. He walked to the firing lane, pointed to the paper target hanging down range on its metal clip. "Mind if I take a look?" he asked.

"Go ahead."

Chris pressed the target recovery button on the wall

of the lane. With a whir the target advanced along its pulley line, flapping back and forth as it traveled up to the front of the shooting stall. Chris unclipped the paper target and examined the holes. The target was torn in the middle. An irregular-shaped hole an inch in diameter occupied the center. Little of the innermost black circle remained. "Nice grouping," he said. "How many shots?"

"Eight."

"From what distance?"

"Law enforcement standard," Jordan replied. "One-hundred and fifty feet."

"I'm impressed," Chris said. He smiled as he looked at the target. "Remind me to never piss you off."

"I'll only shoot at the bad guys. I promise."

He set down the target. "There's something I've been meaning to ask you, Jordan."

"What's that?"

"How are Aiden and Emma coping these days?" Chris asked. "You know, after what happened here?"

Jordan thought of the home invasion and the fight for her life that had occurred within the walls of the estate several years ago. With Chris' help she had been forced to defend her home. Evil had tried to take her family, failed in the attempt, even died here. The incident had made them stronger, closer, their bond unbreakable. "They're fine now" she answered.

"I'm glad," Chris said. "And you?"

"I have my moments," Jordan replied. "Losing my parents and my husband the way I did was hard. I don't think I'll ever fully recover from that."

"One day you will," Chris said. "Time has a tendency to heal even the deepest wounds."

"I suppose so."

"You know I'm here for you and the kids whenever you need me."

"I do."

"Good." He pointed to the ream of paper targets hanging beside the shooting stall. "Mind if I give it a go?"

"Not at all," Jordan said. "Fifty bucks says you don't beat my grouping," she teased.

"Eight rounds?" Chris asked.

"Eight rounds."

"You're on," Chris answered. "Set it up."

Jordan clipped a fresh paper target to the overhead track, pushed the ADVANCE button and sent the target down range.

"You really sure you want to lose fifty bucks?" Chris joked. "I wouldn't want to put you in a position of financial hardship."

"I think I can handle it," Jordan replied.

"I mean, if you're game, we could make it a little more interesting."

With a *click*, the track stopped. The target had reached the end of the range.

"What did you have in mind?"

"Dinner," Chris said. "Salvatore's."

"*Salvatore's?*" Jordan asked. "Fine dining like that will cost you more than fifty bucks. More like two-hundred-and-fifty."

"I'm good for it," Chris said. "Besides, this will be a walk in the park. Fastest fifty I ever made."

"You think so?"

"Undoubtedly."

"You sound pretty confidant for a guy who's about to pay for dinner."

"Just put on your eyes and ears and stand back," Chris said.

Jordan smiled. She put on her shooter's safety glasses and ear protection.

"Clear?" Chris called out.

"Clear," Jordan replied.

"Range is hot," Chris said. He removed his service weapon, took aim, fired off eight quick bursts, then returned the weapon to its holster and pressed the target RETURN button.

The agents waited for the target to reach the front of the shooting stall. "You sure you don't want to spring for McDonald's instead?" Jordan asked.

"Very funny," Chris replied.

When the target was halfway up the lane Jordan said, "I'll even settle for Denny's."

"Prepare to be schooled," Chris teased. The target approached.

"Last chance, Hanover," Jordan said. "Outback Steak House. Final offer."

The target reached the front of the stall. Chris unclipped the paper sheet and presented it to Jordan. "What did I tell you?" he said. "Check it out. Eight shots. All within a half-inch grouping."

"Seven shots," Jordan replied.

"Say what?"

Jordan held the target up to the light. One round had passed through the white ring surrounding the bullseye. "Seven in the middle, one outside."

"Damn."

"You lose," Jordan said. "Tell you what. Rather than save you the embarrassment of asking me to go two out of three I'll let you take me out anyway."

"So you're saying this is a *mercy* dinner."

"In a manner of speaking, yes."

Chris laughed. "That works for me. But I'm still paying."

"Damn right you are," Jordan teased. "You still lost the bet."

"And you're never going to let me forget it, are you?"

Jordan smiled. "Probably not."

Chris laughed. "Salvatore's it is," he said.

Jordan suddenly felt weak. She steadied herself against the shooters stand.

Chris grabbed her by the arm. "Jordan? You okay?"

The psychic impression came out of nowhere, caught Jordan off guard. "The children," she said.

"What are you talking about?" Chris asked.

"The children," Jordan repeated. "Have to save the children."

CHAPTER 2

LA FORTUNA, COSTA RICA

COMMANDER BEN EGAN felt the heat of the sun on his neck. He removed a handkerchief from his pocket, wiped away the sweat, and drove the final nail into the top rail of the dilapidated fence post. The physical labor felt good on his body. The return of a favor gave him peace.

He had found this place two days ago, or perhaps it had found him. The DARPA super-soldier had teleported to a location several miles from here, high up in the mountains, and completed his final assignment: the termination of Taras Verenich; the man ultimately responsible for the death of the daughter of his mission handler, Dr. Jason Merrick. The field test of the Channeler and LEEDA projects, for which he was the principal subject, had been an unprecedented success. As a result, the technologies had become fully integrated within him. The supernatural powers he now possessed had made him both the most powerful weapon in the military and the most sought-after rogue government asset on the planet. He knew DARPA would soon send a capture/kill team after him. It was just a matter of time before they found him. Until then, his only priority was to stay alive.

He heard the commotion, looked up, and stared at the man standing behind the main gate on the far side of the property. Two days ago, the man had slowed his car, pulled up alongside Ben as he walked on the dirt road, and asked what an American was doing wandering in the middle of nowhere. Egan lied, told him he was backpacking his way across the country. Asked when he had last eaten, Egan shook his head, said he couldn't remember. There was no denying the man's kind nature. He insisted he accept a ride and offered him a hot meal and a place to stay for the night. The offer was timely, too good to refuse, and Egan graciously accepted. On the drive, the man introduced himself as Hernando Diaz. Their destination was the orphanage of which he was both the founder and administrator: Casa de los Niños, also known as The Children's House.

The voices had become raised. Egan set down the hammer on the top rail and made his way across the compound to investigate the reason for the argument. Four men stood in front of a black Hummer parked outside the main gate. They were big men, enforcer types judging by the look of them. Their leader was a tall, thin man. Egan watched him press his finger into Hernando's chest. Diaz knocked it aside.

Egan called out as he walked past the main building toward the gate. "You boys lost?" he said.

Diaz looked over his shoulder, raised his hand, tried to warn him off.

The thin man muttered something under his breath.

"Sorry," Egan said. "I don't speak Spanish, but I

17

understand asshole fluently. It's time for you gentlemen to leave."

"Please, Mr. Egan," Diaz warned, "this is none of your concern."

"You're right," Egan replied. He reached the gate. "It's not my concern. Which makes me the perfect mediator."

"What's this, Hernando?" the thin man asked. He looked Egan up and down. "You have a new guard dog?"

"Funny," Egan replied. "This coming from a guy who needs backup just to have a conversation."

"I've got this, Ben," Hernando said. "You don't want to get involved with these men."

"Oh, they seem harmless enough," Egan replied. "Ill-mannered perhaps, but harmless."

"Looks can deceive," the thin man said. He flashed his watch. Cartier, solid gold.

"Keep that in mind," Egan replied.

The four men began to walk from the Hummer to the gate.

Egan looked their way, wagged his finger. "Stay," he said.

The thin man raised his hand. The men stopped, awaited further instruction. He turned his attention back to Diaz. "Remember what I said, Hernando. One week." To his men he said, "Let's go."

The men climbed into the Hummer. The thin man seated himself in the back between his two bodyguards. The driver hit the gas, spinning the vehicles tires, spraying dirt and rubble back against them. Egan waved goodbye.

Hernando Diaz was angry. "Why did you do that?" he asked. "Those are dangerous men!"

Egan watched the Hummer disappear down the road in a cloud of dust. "They don't seem that tough," he replied.

"That's because you don't know them," Hernando said. "That man is Diego Mendoza."

"Should that be important to me?"

"He runs Los Paveños, the largest drug cartel in Costa Rica."

"What does a drug lord want from you, Hernando?" Egan asked.

"It's not me he wants," Diaz replied. "It's the children."

"What do you mean?"

Diaz shook his head. "You shouldn't have gotten involved," he said. "You embarrassed Mendoza in front of his men. He won't allow that to go unpunished."

"Let's assume for the moment that I can take care of myself," Egan replied. In the yard, the youngsters played. Their teacher, Marcella Herrara, looked on "Tell me more about Mendoza. What does he want from your kids?"

The children ran past the men as they walked across the yard.

Hernando tried to conceal the anxiety in his voice. "Mendoza approached me several weeks ago and gave me this." The director of the orphanage unbuttoned his shirt pocket and removed a piece of paper. He handed it to Egan.

Egan read the amount of the check. "One million U.S. dollars," he said.

"It's more money than I've seen in my lifetime," Hernando replied.

"Why did he give it to you?"

Diaz explained. "Mendoza was raised in the slums. He is a child of the streets. Los Paveños took him in. They gave him food and shelter and asked for only one thing in exchange."

"Let me guess," Egan said. "Loyalty."

"Precisely," Diaz agreed.

"But what does that have to do with you and the kids?"

"He knows we rely on donations to stay afloat," Hernando replied. "He said the money was a gift for me to use as I saw fit for the benefit of the children. But I know what he really wants."

"And that is?"

"To own us."

"What do you mean?"

"I know how Los Paveños has grown. I've lost kids to them. They're like a cancer. Once they attach themselves to an organization, it begins to metastasize. Soon they own everyone in it. They have dozens of legitimate companies, mostly in the manufacturing sector. But those of us who know better know the truth. All of their operations support one main aim: the manufacture, packaging and distribution of cocaine."

"But this is just an orphanage," Egan said. "You have nothing of value to offer a drug cartel."

"They want to put the children to work packaging their product for street distribution," Hernando explained. "He wants to pay me one million dollars in cash, each month, to give him control of the orphanage and my kids. What you witnessed was me declining his offer for the third week in a row."

"Let me guess," Egan said. "He's not the kind of guy who's accustomed to taking no for an answer."

Hernando shook his head. "No, he is not."

"I can help you," Egan said.

"No, you can't," Hernando said. "No one can. Once Los Paveños sets their sights on you it's only a matter of time before they take over."

Egan put his hand on the old man's shoulder. "I don't believe for a second you'd allow that to happen, Hernando."

"I'm only one man, Mr. Egan," Diaz said. His voice broke. "I know that at the end of the day I'm powerless to stop them. I don't care what happens to me, but I'd lay down my life to protect the children in my care."

"It will never come to that," Egan replied.

"What do you mean?"

"There's much you don't know about me. Let's just say I possess a certain skill set that is well-suited to dealing with a situation like this."

Diaz was curious. "What do you mean?"

Egan shook his head. "I can't tell you that."

Hernando stepped back. "Tell me the truth, Ben.

You're not just wandering across the country. Who are you? Where did you come from?"

"I'm just a guy repaying a favor, Hernando," Egan replied.

"And your past?" Hernando asked.

Egan smiled. "I'm afraid that's classified."

CHAPTER 3

JAMES MOORE WAS LAYING comfortably in his La-Z-Boy recliner in the living room of his Sarasota Florida home when something shattered the bay window and fell to the floor beside him. The *boom* that followed caused him to throw himself out of the chair and clamp his hands over his ears. The sound of the exploding concussion grenade was deafening, the ringing in his ears unlike anything he had ever experienced before. His first thought was for the safety of his wife, Yvonne. As he clambered to his feet and stumbled toward the kitchen in search of her a second boom erupted, this one coming from the front entrance to his modest two-story home, followed by the shuffling of boots over the linoleum floor and the yelling of commands issued with practiced authority: "Contact, front!" one man called out. "Clear, left!" said another. Then, "Contact, right!" They were yelling at him now. Three men pushed him down, then stood over him, their tactical rifles pointed at his head. "Stay down!" they demanded. "Don't you fucking move!"

This was no break-in, no home invasion. These men were highly trained U.S. military commandos.

What in God's name was a special operations unit doing in his home?

Yvonne screamed.

More yelling, coming from the basement now.

His son was downstairs.

Tommy!

"Don't you dare hurt my son!" Moore screamed as a second assault team raced past him, cleared the doorway and descended the stairs. He struggled as one of the soldier's zip-cuffed his hands behind his back then dragged him to his feet. "What the hell is the meaning of this?"

More yelling in the basement. "Down! Down! Down!" He heard the men come up the stairs, watched them as they dragged his son through the doorway and around the corner into the living room and threw him on the couch.

The soldier that had taken him into custody spoke into the microphone secured around his throat. "Delta One to Command," he heard him say. "Location secure. Three contained. No sign of the package."

"What package?" James yelled.

"The computer files," the soldier replied.

"What computer files?"

Colonel Hallier entered the premises. "Sir," the soldier said. "We can't find a computer anywhere on the premises."

"Tear this place down to the goddamn studs," Hallier demanded. "Find it."

"Copy that, sir."

"Wait!" James yelled. He glared at Hallier. "Sir, please tell me what this is all about? Why are you here? What computer files are you talking about?"

"I have neither the time nor the patience for games, Moore," Hallier replied. "You're in the middle of one hell of a shit storm. If I were you, I'd start cooperating right goddamn now."

"I don't know what you're talking about," James yelled. "Where's my wife? *Yvonne!*"

"Separate them," Hallier commanded. "Take the woman outside."

"Yes, sir," the commando replied.

Yvonne Moore was hysterical. She screamed as the soldier grabbed her by the arm. "God, no!"

"Hurt her and I swear to God I'll kill you!" Moore yelled at the commando as he watched the man escort his wife from their home.

"You're in no position to make threats," Hallier said.

"Are you kidding me?" James yelled. "You break into my home, manhandle my wife and son, and you expect me to be *polite?* Are you out of your fucking mind?"

"Where is Project Channeler and LEEDA?" Hallier asked.

"Project what and what?"

"The computer files you downloaded from Dynamic Life Sciences."

"I didn't download any…"

"Dad," Tommy interrupted.

"Be quiet, Tommy," his father said. "I'll handle this."

"But Dad…"

"Tommy, be quiet!"

Hallier walked over to the teenager, stared down at the boy. "Is there something you want to tell me son?"

Tommy dropped his head. "Yes, sir."

"Come on," Hallier said. "Out with it."

Tommy looked down at his jeans. "Front left pocket," he said. "They're on a flash drive."

James Moore stared at his son in disbelief. "You know about this?" he said. "What the hell did you do?"

"Nothing much. I was just messing around."

"For Christ's sake, Tommy!" his father yelled. "Do you think these men are here because you were just *messing around*?"

"Stand him up," Hallier demanded. "Check his pocket."

The commando retrieved the flash drive, handed it to Hallier.

"Is this the only copy?" Hallier asked.

Tommy stared down at the floor. "Yes, sir," he said.

"How old are you, son?"

"Fifteen, sir."

"Do you have any idea what you've done?"

"It was just for fun," Tommy replied.

"Playing Xbox is fun, son," Hallier said. "You compromised the data centre of a top-secret government installation. That makes you one of three things: stupid, lucky, or goddamn brilliant. I haven't yet decided which it is."

"Ask me for my opinion," James Moore said. He yelled at his son. "Thomas Adam Moore, you will tell these men everything they need to know. Do you understand me? *Everything!*"

"Yes, sir," Tommy replied. He remembered his friend Billy's words… *'we're talking lock-the-door-and-throw-away-the-key jail time, man.'* He was really scared now, on the verge of tears. Jail was for hardened criminals, not a fifteen-year-old computer hacker like himself.

"Start talking," Hallier said.

Tommy explained the hack. "I created a toolset and found a backdoor into the system using a COM interface and my web browser. The toolset created batch scripts to install a persistence protocol. It was then a simple matter of connecting to Dynamic Life Sciences database, querying the system, finding the files and dumping the data from the database to a temp file which I then copied to the flash drive. I could have bought a stolen VPN certificate on the Dark Web if I wanted to, which probably would also have done the trick. Truth is, your network isn't nearly as secure as you think it is. Actually, it sucks."

"How old did you say you were?" Hallier asked.

"Fifteen, sir."

Hallier shook his head. "Brilliant. And stupid."

"Yes, sir."

"You're coming with us. So are your parents. No one is getting released until I know for certain who is and isn't involved in this."

"My parents had no clue about this, sir," Tommy said urgently. "This is all on me, not on them."

"Son," Hallier replied, "for the love of all that's Holy

you'd better be telling me the truth."

"I am, sir."

Hallier turned to the commando. "Take them to DARPA. I want extensive interviews conducted on the family."

"Copy that, sir." The soldier helped Tommy up from the coach. "Let's go," he said.

Tommy turned to Hallier. "Are we under arrest, sir?"

Hallier stared at the flash drive in his hand then back at the boy. "What do you think?" he replied.

CHAPTER 4

"ARE YOU ALL RIGHT?" Chris asked. He helped Jordan to a chair in the Training Room, brought her a bottle of water.

Jordan nodded. "I had a vision," she replied. "It was incredibly strong."

"I'll say," Chris said. "The last time you reacted like that was when you made a connection at the Rosenfeld murder scene."

"The energy felt similar," Jordan agreed. She sipped the water, calmed her breathing.

"Similar how?" Chris asked.

"It's hard to describe. Like I was traveling through a tunnel of bright light at warp speed, then total clarity. That's when I saw them running."

"Who?"

"The children," Jordan replied. "Many of them. They were terrified, running from someone... or something."

"Could you see who or what it was?"

Jordan shook her head. "No, but I know who they were with."

"Who?"

"Commander Egan."

Hanover stared at his partner. "You saw him?"

Jordan nodded. "He's alive. I connected with him again after the attack at Long Beach."

"What do you mean?"

Jordan stood. She was feeling better. The psychic event had passed. "Come with me," she said. "There's something I need to show you."

In the library, Jordan removed a Chinese puzzle box from the mantle and opened it, careful not to touch its contents. "Recognize this?" she asked.

Chris looked at the small piece of plastic. "It's a needle sheath," he said.

Jordan nodded. "I recovered it from the floor of the Pyramid at the Long Beach Campus after it fell."

"Where Merrick's body was found."

"Yes. And the last place Commander Egan was seen alive."

"What happened that day was impossible," Chris recalled. "If I hadn't witnessed it with my own eyes, I'd never have believed it. Egan should have been under that debris pile with Merrick, but he wasn't. There was a pink glow from beneath the rubble before we got to him, then he was gone. He'd vanished into thin air."

"That's right," Jordan said, "and I believe an examination of the trace contents inside this sheath will explain how he could do it."

"What do you mean?"

"Remember what happened to me when I first picked it up?"

Chris nodded. "A drop of the solution absorbed into your skin. It knocked you out."

"That's right," Jordan said. "Then I traveled. To

where, I don't know. Still don't."

"You scared the hell out of me that day," Chris said. "I thought I was going to lose you."

Jordan smiled. "No such luck."

"You said you *connected* with Egan. What do you mean?"

"I saw a jungle path and a waterfall. Egan was on the path. He warned me not to follow him."

"That's probably good advice. He's DARPA's problem now. Let them deal with him."

"It's the children I'm concerned about."

"But you don't know where they are or how to find them. There's nothing you can do, Jordan."

"Maybe there is."

"What do you mean?"

Jordan held up the puzzle box, displayed the needle sheath within it. "I can travel. Like I did before."

Chris understood what she meant. "Are you out of your mind? You know what happened the last time."

"Yes, but you're here with me. If anything goes wrong…"

"Like what?" Chris interrupted. "Like you go into cardiac arrest? Exposing yourself to that stuff again could send you on some psychic trip from which you might not return. No, Jordan. You can't do it. It's far too dangerous. You have no idea how repeated exposure to whatever the hell is in that thing will affect you. Besides, that sheath is evidence. You should have surrendered it to DARPA, given it to Hallier."

"I'm used to it now. I'll be fine."

"Don't do it, Jordan," Chris warned.

Jordan removed the plastic sheath from the puzzle box. "I know what I'm doing, Chris."

"Jordan…"

"Trust me."

Jordan placed the needle sheath in her palm, closed her eyes, and thought about the children. The mild vibration she felt in her hand soon extended throughout her entire body.

"Jordan," Chris said, "can you hear me?" He wanted to touch her, shake her, break the connection the strange matter was having on her, but he was afraid of whatever repercussions such an action might bring. She was somewhere else now, on a plane of existence he did not understand and could not follow, in a place between this world and the next. All he could do was wait for the events to take their course and be there for her when she returned.

Jordan traveled. When she opened her eyes a few seconds later, she found herself standing in the middle of a well-trodden path. She could feel the warmth of the sun on her body and smell the fresh mountain air. She was surrounded by lush tropical plants. Nearby, she heard the sound of a waterfall and the voices of children. Jordan walked along the narrow path until she reached the edge of a clearing. In the distance she saw a compound: several large buildings surrounded by a wood and wire fence. As she approached the perimeter of the property in her dream-like state her hearing

32

became hyper-focused. Jordan zeroed-in on a group of men standing at the edge of the forest, all heavily armed. She watched as a tall thin man, dressed in camouflage from head to toe, approached the leader of what appeared to be an assault team. Jordan listened to the men as they talked.

"Status report," the thin man asked.

"Diaz and the woman are inside the main building with the children," the man said.

"Bring him to me."

"And the woman?"

"Do what you want with her."

"Yes, sir."

"What about the American?"

"No one has seen him."

"Keep watch. He'll be back. If he causes trouble, kill him."

"Yes, sir."

"When does the shipment arrive?"

"Within the hour."

"Good. Organize the children. Make sure they have it packaged and ready for transport by tonight."

"Yes, sir."

"Send in your men. Get the old man. Do it now."

"Yes, sir." The sentry spoke to his men, pointed to the compound, issued instructions.

The thin man walked away.

In the distance, a figure stood beyond the tree line, hidden in the forest.

Unable to maintain her hold on the ethereal plane,

the connection began to fade. As fast as she had traveled to the location of the children, Jordan was pulled back through the mysterious portal in her mind to the safety and security of the library. She drew a deep breath and stared at Chris.

Chris took her hand, spoke to her. "Jordan, are you all right?"

Jordan nodded. "How long was I gone?" she asked.

"A few seconds."

"It seemed longer."

"It was long enough for me."

"I heard them."

"Heard who?"

"The children."

"Where are they?"

"I don't know. But they're in trouble. He's going to hurt them if they don't do what he says."

"Who is?"

"The thin man."

CHAPTER 5

WITH THE DEPARTURE of Diego Mendoza and his men, Ben Egan returned to the job of mending the broken fence. The visit from the drug lord had upset Hernando Diaz, who had retired to his office to work and take his mind off the confrontation. In the playground, Marcella Herrara sat on the ground with the youngest child in the orphanage, Teresa Gomez. The little girl was having difficulty breathing. Marcella rubbed her back, comforted her.

"Remember what I told you to do?" Marcella said.

"Take s-slow, d-deep breaths," Teresa replied.

"That's right."

"My chest hurts."

"I know it does, sweetie."

"H-how come?"

"Because you have a medical condition," Marcella said as she stroked her hair. "It's called asthma. Do you need your puffer?"

Teresa shook her head. She tried to control her breathing. "I can manage," the girl said. She opened her mouth and inhaled tentatively at first, then graduated to fuller, deeper breaths.

Marcella gave her a hug. "That's my girl," she said. "Do you want to lay down for a while?"

"It always helps," Teresa replied.

"Then off you go," her teacher said.

Marcella helped the child to her feet. She watched as she walked off in the direction of the dormitory.

Egan called out from across the compound. "Everything all right, Marcella?"

Marcella turned around, smiled and waved. "Just a minor medical emergency," she said. She walked over to Egan.

"Is she going to be okay?" Ben asked.

Marcella nodded. "She will be. It happens at least once a day. Nothing I can't deal with."

Ben smiled. "School teacher *and* doctor. You're a person of many talents."

"As are you," Marcella replied. "I saw how you handled those men at the gate."

Egan shrugged. "It was no big deal."

"Actually, it was. Hernando has been worried about them for a while, of what the repercussions of turning them down might be."

"He told you what they want?"

"He tells me everything," Marcella replied. "He has to. There's just the two of us here to run the entire facility and take care of the children. We can't afford to keep secrets from each other."

"How many kids are here?" Egan asked.

"Nine."

"How old?"

"Teresa, the little one you saw me helping, is four. The rest are older. They range in age from six to ten."

"So young," Ben said. "How did they end up here?"

"Los Paveños, mostly," Marcella said. "Their parents either worked for or were killed by the cartel. With no one to care for them they became orphans, children of the street. Local churches search for them. When a child is found they bring them here."

"Jesus," Egan replied.

Marcella nodded. "It wasn't always this way. This used to be a good place to live. Mostly it still is. But there is not a lot of opportunity here. Many families barely survive. Some can't afford to feed their children. They see friends and neighbors who once were suffering like them now driving fancy new cars, flashing money all over town, dining out at expensive restaurants, sending their children to private schools. No one asks where the money comes from. Everyone knows its cartel cash. And no one will say a thing for fear of being killed. Which is exactly what happened to the parents of these children."

"Hasn't your government tried to stop it?"

Marcella shrugged. "They do what they can. But for every person who dies working for the cartel there's another waiting to take their place. It's a vicious circle. The children are left to grow up here. We do the best we can, but we know it will never really be home. And they know it too."

"But surely your adoption rates are high."

Marcella shook her head. "This is not a place to which prospective parents want to travel to adopt a child. It's too dangerous. Kidnappings are rare, but they occur."

"So the children pay the price."

"Yes, they do."

"How do you cope with the pressure?" Egan asked.

"We can't anymore. We've been making plans."

"Such as?"

"To take the children and leave."

"And go where?"

"We're not sure yet," Marcella said. "A church in San Jose has offered to take us in. But they can only offer us temporary accommodations. We won't do that to the children. They've been through enough already. No, if we're going to move it will be somewhere where they will be safe. Somewhere Los Paveños can't get to them."

Egan shook his head. "This just isn't right."

"Right or wrong, Mr. Egan, it is our reality."

"The little girl, Teresa. How long has she been sick?"

"Since she arrived here. That was a year ago."

"Is she receiving treatment?"

"It's inconsistent. A friend of mine is a doctor. He gives us the expired medications his patients turn in to the clinic, physician's samples, bottles of aspirin and ibuprofen, Band-Aids, ointment, gauze, and so on. He's supposed to dispose of the drugs, but he looks the other way. He knows how badly the children need them. We're fortunate. Except for Teresa, they're all healthy."

"They're lucky to have such responsible caregivers," Egan said.

Marcella smiled. "Thank you."

Hernando suddenly appeared in the dormitory

doorway. "Marcella," he called out. "Come quickly. It's Teresa. She can't breathe!"

Marcella ran across the compound. Egan followed.

Inside, the girl was sitting up in her bed, clutching her chest. Her body was shaking. "C-can't breathe," she said. "H-help... me."

"Has this happened before?" Egan asked.

"No," Marcella replied. She rifled through the girl's bedside table.

"What are you looking for?" Hernando asked.

"Her inhaler," Marcella said. "Blue cover and cap. Where is it?"

Hernando checked the floor and under the bed. "I can't find it. Wait... there. In the wastebasket."

"God, no!" Marcella said. She retrieved the puffer from the trash can, pulled off the cover, placed it in the child's mouth, tried to dispense a measured dose of the life-saving medication.

Empty.

Marcella yelled at Hernando. "The medicine cabinet... quickly!"

Hernando raced across the room, threw open the cabinet door, looked for the special box marked TERESA RX, opened the lid.

Empty.

He turned to Marcella; his face ashen. "Nothing," he said. "That was the last one. She has no medication left. It's all gone."

The girl fell back on the bed.

Her breathing had stopped. Her airway was now

fully obstructed.

"No!" Marcella cried. "Not this girl! Not this sweet, sweet girl!" She picked up Teresa in her arms. The girl was limp. Her arms fell to her sides.

"Put her down," Egan said.

Through her tears, Marcella said, "What?"

"Quickly," Egan said. "Lay her down. Step aside."

"What are you going to…"

"Just do it!"

Marcella lay the girl's head gently down on the pillow. "I'm sorry, Teresa," she cried. "I'm so, so sorry."

Egan placed his hand on the girl's chest, closed his eyes, and concentrated.

"What are you doing?" Hernando asked.

Egan said nothing. Beneath his hand, the small child's body began to quiver, then shake. A strange glow, rose-red, emanated from the palm of his hand. The air in the room suddenly felt electrified, as if the incomprehensible force field Egan was exerting upon the girl was being carried on every air molecule.

The girl's chest slowly began to rise and fall. She opened her eyes.

Her breathing returned to normal.

Egan removed his hand from her chest. "Hey, sweetie," he said. "You okay?"

The girl stared at him, nodded her head. "I feel strange," she said.

"What do you mean, baby?" Marcella asked.

The little girl forced a smile. "The pain in my chest.

It's gone."

Egan smiled. "You're going to be fine," he said. "Just lay here and rest up for a while, okay?"

"Okay," Teresa replied.

Egan stood. Hernando and Marcella stared at him in disbelief.

"What?" Egan said. He smiled. "You mean *you* can't do that?"

"I've never seen anything like that in my life," Hernando said.

Marcella was aghast. "Impossible," she said. "Absolutely impossible."

Hernando began to speak. "How did you…"

Egan raised his hand. "It was nothing."

"You healed her with your touch," Marcella said. "I can't believe you just did that."

"I couldn't stand by and watch the girl die," Egan said. "Not when I knew I could help."

"I don't know what to say," Hernando said. "I'm speechless."

"And that's exactly how it has to stay," Egan said. "Neither of you can tell a soul about what you saw here today. If you do your lives could be in danger. Do you understand?"

"Yes," Hernando said.

"Of course," Marcella agreed.

Egan looked down at the young girl. She was asleep now. Her breathing was normal. Her chest rose and fell softly. "Her asthma is gone," he said. "Her respiratory system is as healthy as yours or mine."

"How can we possibly repay you for what you've done for her?" Hernando asked.

Egan put his hand on the man's shoulder. "There is one thing I can think of," he said.

"Name it," Hernando said.

"Let me deal with Los Paveños."

CHAPTER 6

COLONEL QUENTIN HALLIER stared at the scientists seated around the conference table. "What's the consensus," he asked. "Is it all there?"

Dr. Nicholas Ginzberg and his research team from Dynamic Life Sciences had spent the last few hours pouring through the printouts downloaded from the flash drive the assault team had secured from young Tommy Moore. Two binders were marked TOP SECRET: EYES ONLY. The first was labeled Project Channeler, the second Project LEEDA. The lead scientist conferred with his colleagues, then nodded. "Yes, Colonel," he said. "The data appear to be complete."

"And the formulas?"

"The science looks good," Ginzberg replied. "We'll need to recreate them in the lab to be sure."

"How soon can you get started?" Hallier asked.

Ginzberg looked puzzled. "Forgive me, Colonel," he said, "but I thought you said everything to do with our work at DLS had been scrubbed. Those were your last orders."

Hallier nodded. "That was before we regained control of these files. The situation has changed."

"Very well," Ginzberg replied. "How do you want us to proceed?"

"I'm tasking you and your team with two primary objectives," Hallier said. "First, recreate the formulas for Channeler and LEEDA."

The doctors nodded. "That won't be a problem," Ginzberg answered. "And the second?"

"Get me the antidotes for both technologies," Hallier replied.

"Already done, sir," Ginzberg said.

"You have them?" Hallier asked.

Ginzberg nodded. "They're a mandatory part of the formulation process intended to be deployed as a counteragent in the event of an emergency," the scientist replied. "Based on the depth and the breadth of PROJECT GENESIS we created a single antidote to counteract the combined effects of Channeler and LEEDA. We call it ACHILLES."

"Is it weaponized?"

"Yes, sir," Ginzberg answered. "Achilles is delivered as a gas. Once inhaled by the target, it instantly reverses the biological effects of Channeler and LEEDA."

"How long will it last?"

"Permanently, sir."

"I need Achilles immediately," Hallier said.

The men looked concerned.

"Is that a problem, Doctor?"

Ginzberg spoke tentatively. "Sir, Achilles and all of our counteragents are locked in a bomb-proof vault at DLS. But the lab has been shuttered. How are we supposed to gain access to it?"

"Consider yourselves back in business," Hallier said. "Security is reopening the facility as we speak. You have carte blanche to continue your research. Whatever you'll need, it's yours."

"Thank you, Colonel," Ginzberg replied.

Hallier addressed the table sternly. "I'm not being benevolent, doctors," he said. "This situation requires your undivided attention. You're to get me Achilles and pursue the re-creation of Channeler and LEEDA around the clock. As of this moment your life goes on hold. Your families will be notified accordingly. You'll eat and sleep at DLS until this is finished. I need results, and I need them fast."

Hallier stood. "Transportation is ready and waiting for you. I suggest you get started the minute you arrive."

The men rose from their chairs. "Yes, sir," Ginzberg replied.

∞ ∞ ∞

Hallier waited for the guard to unlock the interrogation room door. He entered the small room. Tommy Moore sat in the chair, feet curled under him, arms wrapped around his legs. He looked up. "Where are my parents?" he asked.

"Down the hall," Hallier answered.

"They okay?"

"You mean besides being thoroughly upset with you?" Hallier replied. "Yes, they're fine."

"They knew nothing about this."

"I know."

Tommy seemed surprised. "You do?"

Hallier sat on the corner of the desk, looked at the teen. "Your parents seem like very nice people, Tommy. If you haven't already guessed by now, we're damn good at what we do around here. If they were lying to us about any of this, we'd know it."

"Are you going to let them go?" the teen asked.

"I see no reason to hold them," Hallier said. "You, on the other hand, might be here for a while. That is if you decline my offer."

Tommy sat up. "What offer?"

"Remember what I said to you at your home?" Hallier asked.

"No, sir," Tommy answered. "To be honest, I was too busy trying not to wet myself."

Hallier forced a smile. "Special operator raids have that effect on people," he replied. "I said you had to be stupid, lucky or brilliant to hack us like you did."

"Yes, sir," Tommy said.

"Do you know how many levels of security we have in place to keep people like you from gaining access to our data?"

"A lot?"

"That's right," Hallier said. "And you circumvented each and every one of them. Which tells me you didn't hack into us by sheer accident or get lucky. And you're sure as hell not stupid. So that leaves brilliant. You're a hacking prodigy, aren't you?"

"To be honest, sir," Tommy answered, "there's not

much about computer security systems I don't know."

"I figured as much," Hallier said. He leaned back in his chair. "You've put me in a very difficult position, Mr. Moore."

"I won't do it again," Tommy said.

"I can charge you…" Hallier began.

"I promise!"

"… which would destroy your life and pretty much any hope for a decent future you could have…"

Tommy pleaded. "I swear to God!"

"… or I could look the other way on this and put you to work for me."

Dumbfounded, Tommy stared at the colonel. "Huh?" he said.

"You heard me," Hallier said. "You come to work for DARPA. With your parent's permission, of course. But there's a catch."

Tommy was stunned. "What catch?" he asked.

"No one can know," Hallier said. "Not your schoolmates, your teachers… not even your best friend. That's a lot of responsibility to place on the shoulders of most adults, much less a fifteen-year-old boy. So, the question remains."

"Sir?" Tommy asked nervously.

"Do you think you can handle it?"

Tommy didn't bat an eye. He nodded. "Yes, sir!"

"I thought so," Hallier said.

"What do you need me to do?" Tommy asked.

"Nothing for now," Hallier said. "You'll go back home with your parents. We'll provide you with an encrypted laptop which you'll use for any assignments we send to you. There's one more condition."

"Name it."

"You don't black hat or otherwise hack another website ever again. The second you do this offer is rescinded, permanently."

"I won't, sir."

"Good," Hallier said. He extended his hand. "Welcome to DARPA, Mr. Moore."

Tommy smiled. He shook the colonel's hand. "Thank you, sir. I won't let you down."

"No, you won't," Hallier replied firmly. "You ready to go see your parents now?"

"Yes, please, Colonel."

"All right," Hallier said.

"They're not gonna believe this," Tommy said excitedly. "Me, working for the Department of Defense."

"As a *civilian* contractor, Mr. Moore. Nothing more."

"Yes, sir. But you've got to admit it."

"Admit what?" Hallier asked.

"It's really frickin' cool!"

Hallier forced back a smile. He opened the interrogation room door for Tommy. "Go see your parents," he said. "Down the hall, second door on your right."

"Thank you, sir," Tommy replied. He left the room and hustled down the hallway.

Hallier closed the door. He walked to the corner of

the room, lifted a telephone handset from its cradle, and placed a call.

"General Ford's office."

"Colonel Quentin Hallier for General Ford."

"One moment, Colonel," the secretary replied.

Ford picked up the call. "How can I help you, Colonel?"

"Sir, I'm calling regarding projects Channeler and LEEDA."

"There's nothing to discuss, Colonel," Ford replied. "They're shut down. DLS is dead. So is GENESIS."

"With respect, sir, there's been a development. We've been able to recover the files."

"How is that possible?" Ford asked. "You said the EMP took out everything... that there were no backups."

"That was our initial assessment of the situation, sir. We've since been able to secure the data from an outside source. One not previously available to us."

"What about Commander Egan?"

"With your permission, sir, I'd like to assemble a special ops team to track him down."

"How?" Ford asked. "He has no biomarkers. He's a ghost."

"I may have a solution, sir," Hallier replied. "It's unconventional, but I think it might work."

"I don't care what you have to do, Colonel," Ford said. "Egan's off his leash, and we both know the risk that poses to national security."

"Yes, sir."

"All right," Ford said. "You can proceed. But do it fast. Find him and bring him in, one way or the other."

"Copy that, sir."

Ford hung up.

Hallier placed a second call.

"Federal Bureau of Investigation."

"Assistant Director Ann Ridgeway," Hallier said.

"Please hold."

The call was picked up seconds later. "This is Ridgeway."

"Ann, it's Quentin."

"Good afternoon, Colonel," the Assistant Director said. "To what do I owe the pleasure?"

"I need your help."

"Of course. What can I do for you?"

"I need to speak with Agent Quest," Hallier said. "It's an emergency."

CHAPTER 7

"TELL ME WHAT HAPPENED, JORDAN," Chris asked. "What did you see? Who is the thin man?"

Jordan sat back in her chair. "I don't know," she said, "but he seems to be in charge."

"Of what?"

"Some kind of tactical operation. But it doesn't feel military."

"What do they have to do with the children?" Chris asked.

Jordan recalled the details of the conversation she had overheard in the jungle. "He wants to put them to work," Jordan replied. "Some kind of forced labor."

"Where are they?"

"I'm not sure," Jordan said. "But I know it's nowhere close by." Jordan stared at the needle sheath in her hand. "Commander Egan is with them. The energy signature from the needle cover is a direct connection to him."

"You saw him?"

"Not exactly," Jordan replied. "But I felt him there, in the distance, out of sight, watching the men."

"Did he see you?" Chris asked.

Jordan shook her head. "I don't think so."

Chris stood. He walked around the room, considered the magnitude of what Jordan had just told him. "You know what this means, right?"

Jordan nodded. She placed the needle sheath back into its secret compartment within the Chinese puzzle box. "Commander Egan is alive."

"More than that," Chris said. "It means that you can track him. DARPA needs to know about this. You need to contact Hallier."

Jordan's cellphone rang. She checked the display: RIDGEWAY. She took the call.

"Good morning, Assistant Director."

"Good morning, Agent Quest. I need you to come to the office as soon as possible."

"Yes, ma'am," Jordan replied. "May I ask what this is about?"

"I just got off the phone with Colonel Hallier from DARPA," ADC Ridgeway replied. "He needs to speak with you right away. He says it's an emergency. Is Agent Hanover with you?"

Jordan stared at Chris. "Yes, ma'am."

"Good. How soon can you both be here?"

"Within the hour, ma'am."

"Very well," Ridgeway said. "I'll be expecting you." She hung up.

"That was Ridgeway," Jordan said. "We have to go in."

"Did she say why?"

"Colonel Hallier needs to speak with me."

"Think this has anything to do with Commander Egan?" Chris asked.

"What other reason would he have to reach out to me?" Jordan asked.

Chris opened the door for Jordan as they left the library. "That's a very good question," he said.

"My car or yours?" Jordan said.

"You look better in your Maserati than you do in my Camry," Chris joked.

Jordan laughed. "My wheels it is." She hugged Marissa and kissed her children goodbye. Lucy followed them to the door.

"Mind if I drive?" Chris asked.

Jordan smiled. "Not a chance."

Jordan drove through the gates of the mansion, waited for them to close behind her, then rounded the corner. A gray sedan was parked down the street. Jordan caught a glimpse of the driver. Through the tinted windows she could make out the profile of a man talking on his cell phone. Jordan checked her rear-view mirror as she drove past.

Chris took notice. "What's up?" he asked.

Jordan shook her head. "It's nothing."

"Something caught your attention," Chris pressed. "What is it?"

"The car back there," Jordan said. "Something about it feels wrong."

Chris shrugged. "Since when is it illegal for a guy to stop and make a phone call?"

Jordan nodded. "You're right," she said. "Forget it."

"I know what you're thinking, Jordan," Chris said. "But it's been years since the home invasion. Everything's good now. The bad guys are dead. You,

Marissa and the kids are all safe now."

"I know," Jordan replied. "I guess the fear will never be entirely gone, no matter how hard I try."

"Considering what you and your family went through that's understandable," Chris said. He took out his cellphone. "If it will make you feel any better, I'll call it in. The local cops can swing by and check him out."

"That's okay," Jordan replied. "It's just me. I need to get over it."

"You sure?"

"Positive."

"Good enough," Chris said. He smiled. "Sure you won't let me drive?"

Jordan laughed. "One-hundred percent."

The man parked in the gray sedan waited until the Maserati had driven down the street and rounded the corner. From his jacket pocket he removed a notepad, checked his watch and recorded the time. His picked up the mini binoculars from the passenger seat beside him, turned his attention back to the mansion, focused the lenses and panned the windows of the estate. He watched the housekeeper as she removed crystal glasses from a rosewood hutch, set them on the dining room table and began to polish each piece. The girl was in the library. He could not locate the boy or the dog.

This was his third week watching the family. He had staggered the dates and times so as not to arouse suspicion and changed surveillance vehicles frequently.

Last week, he had rented a truck from a moving company and parked in front of a house for sale adjacent to the Quest estate. The week before his vehicle of choice had been a cargo van which he had disguised with magnetic signage to appear to be in the pest control business. His last visit had been eight o'clock yesterday morning. Red Honda Civic. He'd watched the housekeeper pull out of the garage, then followed her from a distance as she drove the children to school. He knew their names: Emma and Aiden. The dog was Lucy. The housekeeper was Marissa. There was a private security detail. He observed their operatives as they followed Marissa whenever she traveled with the children. They shouldn't be a problem. He had plenty of experience dealing with such individuals. When he wanted to get to the children, he would.

A black SUV rounded the corner at the foot of the street. The security detail. He had seen the vehicle before at the school, recognized it immediately.

He slipped the binoculars into the glove box, started the car, backed into the driveway of the house next door, then pulled out and drove down the street. The SUV slowed as it passed. The tinted windows of the car prevented him from being seen. He knew they had already noted the license plate and make and model of his car. No matter. They would never see it again.

He would be back tomorrow in a different vehicle at a different time, waiting, watching. Eventually, when the moment presented itself, he would act.

CHAPTER 8

"TEQUILA?" HERNANDO DIAZ asked.

"Thank you," Ben Egan replied.

The director of the orphanage turned in his chair, opened the glass doors of the bookcase behind him, and removed a bottle of Jose Cuervo and two small glasses. He poured the drinks, then slid a glass across the desk to Egan.

"What you did for Teresa was incredible," Hernando said. "How did you do it?"

Egan sipped the drink, considered his response. "I was born with the ability," he lied. "It's a gift."

Diaz nodded. "I've heard of such things," he said, "but I thought they were the stuff of movies. Today you proved that isn't so. You are a miracle man, Mr. Egan. A gifted healer."

Egan thought of the chaos and destruction he and the late Dr. Jason Merrick had brought to the University of Southern California's Long Beach Campus days earlier and the death of Taras Verenich, whom he had murdered after teleporting to Costa Rica from the University. He was anything but a gifted healer. Back in the United States he was a DARPA super-soldier, a trained assassin, the living embodiment of the GENESIS project, and now a wanted man. But here in La Fortuna he was merely Ben Egan, an American tourist drifting across the country, living one day to the next. He smiled at his new friend. "Thank you," he replied.

Hernando sighed. "I'm concerned about my kids, Ben."

"How so?" Egan asked.

"I don't think the orphanage can survive for very much longer."

"What do you mean?"

Hernando stood from his desk, walked to his office window, looked outside. Marcella was watching over the children as they played in the yard. "The wolves are at the door," he said, "and they're hungry."

"By wolves I assume you're referring to Los Paveños."

Hernando nodded. "It's getting harder to say no to them."

"You're not referring to the amount of money they're offering, are you?" Egan said.

Hernando turned around. He shook his head. "I don't care about money," he replied sternly. "What I do care about is the safety of Marcella and the children." He walked to his desk, opened his top drawer, took out an envelope, opened it and let the contents spill over his desk. "Eleven bullets," he said. "Marcella found them on the driver's seat of our minivan last week when she took the children into town for the afternoon. Mendoza wants to be sure we get the message: one bullet for me, one for Marcella, and each of the children."

Egan picked up the bullet, examined it. Nine-millimeter. "What I don't understand is why Los

Paveños is so insistent on taking over the orphanage," he said. "Why these kids? What do they have to offer that is so damn important to them?"

"Most of their parents were in the cartel," Hernando replied. "It doesn't matter that they were killed by them. The children were raised by their parents to idolize the narcos, the drug-traffickers. If they weren't here, they'd have been put to work on the streets pedaling drugs long ago. Most of them would probably be dead by now. Here they have hope for a future. There's still a chance a good family might adopt them, give them an education, enable them to live a long and prosperous life. The second the narcos get their hands on them that opportunity ends."

"Can't you go to the police?" Egan asked.

Hernando laughed. "Cartel members outnumber law enforcement twenty to one. Los Paveños knows every move the police are going to make before they make it. Their people are everywhere."

"What steps have you taken to keep you and the children safe?" Egan asked.

"What do you mean?" Hernando said.

"Do you keep a gun on the property?"

Hernando shook his head. "What does an orphanage director need with a gun? No, we do not keep weapons of any kind on the premises. I have no use for such dangerous things."

"Maybe it's time you did," Egan said.

"I'm a pacifist, Mr. Egan," Hernando explained. "I don't believe in solving problems using violence. Like

Marcella, I'm also a teacher. That's not the kind of example I want to set for the children."

"There's another lesson you need to consider," Egan said.

"And that would be?"

"Sometimes," Egan said, "when the odds are against you, the only option you have is to defend yourself."

Hernando collected the bullets from the desk, poured them back in the envelope, returned them to the drawer. "Unfortunately, I'm beginning to see that may be true," he replied. "I just don't know where to begin."

"I do," Egan said.

"What did you have in mind?"

"I need you to set up a meeting."

"With whom?"

"Diego Mendoza."

"What for?"

"To make peace."

Hernando leaned back, folded his arms. "Are you insane?"

Egan smiled. "Trust me," he said. "I know what I'm doing."

"You don't know Diego Mendoza like I do," Hernando replied. "He is not a reasonable man. He won't listen to a word you have to say. Quite frankly, he'll probably shoot you dead on the spot just to prove that he mustn't be crossed."

"This might be difficult for you to believe, Hernando," Egan said, "but I'm a very hard man to kill."

The director stared at Egan. "Somehow I believe

that," he said.

"How soon can you reach out to Mendoza?" Egan asked.

"I can travel into town this afternoon," Hernando said. "Like I said, he has people everywhere. I know where to find his lieutenants."

"Good," Egan said. "Tell them you're ready to discuss his offer. I'll take it from there."

Hernando placed his head in his hands, let out a heavy sigh. "I'm worried about this, Mr. Egan. Mendoza is unpredictable."

"So am I," Egan said.

"What if he refuses to meet with me?"

"He won't. Men like that take great satisfaction in controlling others. He'll think he's finally gotten to you."

"And then?" Hernando asked.

"Then he's mine."

CHAPTER 9

HAVING FOUND NO EVIDENCE of their involvement in the unlawful activities of their son and been given every assurance that young Tommy's online activity would be closely monitored, Hallier released the Moore family and permitted them to return to their Florida home. One day, when the need arose, he would call upon the teenage computer genius to assist him in matters pertaining to national security.

Right now, he was tasked with a more pressing concern: track down Commander Ben Egan and secure his immediate return to the United States to face justice for his crimes against the military and the government.

The scientific team were en route to Dynamic Life Sciences. He would soon have the antidote and formulas needed for the continuation of Projects Channeler and LEEDA. General Ford had made it clear: there would be no further stain on the agency. The super-soldier was to be dealt with by any means necessary. Ben Egan's actions hereon in would dictate his fate or seal his destiny. He would either be taken into custody to face the charges against him or terminated.

Hallier entered the boardroom, then closed and locked the door. He had emailed an encrypted video teleconferencing link to FBI Assistant Director Ann Ridgeway. It was time.

Hallier opened the computer and activated the communications channel. Ann Ridgeway appeared on screen. Special agents Jordan Quest and Chris Hanover were seated beside her.

"Hello Ann, Agents," Hallier said. "Thank you for taking the time to meet with me on such short notice."

"Not a problem, Colonel," Ann Ridgeway said. "How can we help you?"

"It's about Commander Egan," Hallier replied.

"That was quite the disappearing act he pulled at USC Long Beach, Colonel," Chris said. "Agent Quest and I saw him vanish right before our eyes. How was that possible?"

"The answer to that question is top secret," Hallier replied. "Let's just say that he's able to travel anywhere he wants to go, at will."

Chris turned to Jordan. "You were right," he said. "It was Egan you saw. He's alive."

"You've *seen* the commander, Agent Quest?" Hallier asked.

Jordan nodded. "Twice."

Hallier looked stunned. "But how…"

"I was exposed to something in the Pyramid, at the scene where Dr. Merrick's body was found," Jordan said. "The best way to put it is to say that it reacted with my psychic abilities, heightened them. The two worked in concert."

"Do you know where Commander Egan is right now?" Hallier asked.

"Not for certain, no."

"Could you find him if you tried?"

"I believe that would be possible," Jordan replied.

"I was hoping to ask for your help once more," Hallier said. "If you can help us find him, we believe we can neutralize his abilities, turn them off. The problem is that he could be anywhere in the world. And for all of us that presents a very dangerous situation. Commander Egan is a human weapon. As such, his value to foreign governments, friend or foe, is incalculable."

"Then how do you stop him?" ADC Ridgeway asked. "Finding Egan is one thing, but if he can disappear in the blink of an eye…"

Hallier interrupted. "Measures are being taken to ensure that won't happen again, Ann. Our first objective, with Agent Quest's help, is to track him to a specific geographic location. Once that has been accomplished my men will take it from there."

Ann Ridgeway nodded in agreement. "Under the circumstances we'll be pleased to let you borrow Agent Quest."

"Thank you," he replied.

"May I make a request, Colonel?" Jordan asked.

"Name it."

"Agent Hanover and I are a team. I'd prefer it if we both accompanied your men on this assignment. We'll be more effective if we're on scene together."

"Of course," Hallier replied. "I'll make immediate arrangements for your air transportation to DARPA from Joint Forces Training Base Los Alamitos. A plane will be waiting for you when you arrive."

"We're on our way, Colonel," Jordan said.

"Thank you, agents," Hallier replied.

The connection was terminated.

CHAPTER 10

ELTON MANNAFORT WAS guilty as sin, not that it mattered anymore.

The kidnapping case against him had been a lock, the evidence rock-solid. But when the victim upon whom the prosecution had built its case failed to appear in court to testify against him, the charges were dropped. He knew the reason. The bullet that was slipped into the tuna sandwich the mother had prepared for her daughter and which her grade-two teacher had discovered did the trick. The woman had taken the hint and fled with her child. An exhaustive search for the pair had turned up nothing. They had gone into hiding.

No victim, no case.

Life was good.

The abduction had taken place two years ago when the young mother, Carrie Schumacher, had been thoughtful enough to help him load his groceries into the back of his minivan. Unbeknownst to her, both the plaster cast and the sling he wore on his arm had been props. Elton had thanked her for her kind gesture by delivering a brutal blow to the back of her head, which rendered her unconscious, then pushed her into the back of the van. Carrie awoke several hours later, tied to a chair in his cabin in the mountains. She spent the next two weeks irritatingly begging for her life. He had intended to kill her. His desire for new game, coupled with her incessant whining, was getting on his nerves. It was on the walk back to his cabin after digging her grave in the woods that the police tactical team surprised him, took him into custody and rescued Carrie. He later found out how he they had found him: a lead from a famous psychic. Her name was Jordan Quest.

The planning of the abduction had been perfect, its execution flawless. It was to have been his blueprint for many more kidnappings to come. His arrest should never have happened. In the end, the five-thousand dollars it had cost him to plant the bullet turned out to be money well spent. It had secured his freedom and permitted him to put into place a new plan: find and destroy the woman ultimately responsible for his capture.

Elton returned the gray sedan to the car rental agency and took a taxi back to his room at the Manor Inn Apartments. The weekly rental was a dive and belied its name, being as far from a stately manor as one could imagine, but it served the purpose. He entered the third-floor room, locked the door, and peered out the curtain. To his knowledge he had not been followed. With the dismissal of his charges, the police had no further reason to keep him under surveillance. But in Elton's world, the cops were one small step up from the bad guys. If anyone wanted to see proof of that conviction, he'd be happy to show them. His body bore the marks to prove it.

Elton closed the drapes, walked across the room,

opened his jacket pocket, removed a multipurpose screwdriver tool, then dragged a guest chair across the floor and positioned it under the air-conditioning vent. He stood on the chair, opened the device, used the straight screwdriver blade to remove the vent cover screws, tossed the metal grill on the floor, reached inside and pulled out a leather satchel. He jumped down from the chair, sat on the edge of the bed, opened the goody bag and laid out its precious contents: three cloth hoods, mouth gags, duct tape, plastic zip-tie handcuffs, dog treats, a folding knife, Colt nine-millimeter semi-automatic handgun, a map of the Greater Los Angeles area, a pen and a yellow highlighter.

He opened the map. The highlighted streets indicated the most commonly used routes taken by the housekeeper each week. His sidebar notes, based on his observation of her weekly activities, explained the reasons and times for the trips:

Monday-Friday, 8:00 AM: Drops children at school. 3 PM: picks them up.

Monday-Friday, 1-2 PM: Walks dog.

Tuesday/Thursday, 4-5 PM: Aiden; Rising Sun Martial Arts.

Tuesday/Thursday, 4:30 PM-5:30 PM: Emma; Baylor Gymnastics.

Wednesdays, 9:00 AM-12:00 PM: Groceries, sundry tasks.

Monday, Wednesday, Friday 4:00 PM: Home with children.

Tuesday, Thursday, 6:30 PM: Home with children.

Frequently changing cars saw to it that the woman's shadow security detail never saw him. The Ansee digital binoculars he used featured a built-in camera with still photo and video shooting capability. He secretly video-recorded the woman and the children from a distance wherever they went. He reviewed the day's footage: Aiden playing baseball during gym class, Emma having lunch with her friends, Marissa supervising Lucy while she played in the dog park.

When the Quest woman was at home, she spent her time with her family in the estate.

There was one unfortunate variable he could not nail down: the sporadically timed visits of the man he learned was her partner, FBI Special Agent Chris Hanover.

He had thought long and hard about his plan of attack. He would strike when the woman was away, the children separated from the housekeeper. The personal security team would have to be distracted or incapacitated. This would not be a problem.

He returned the items to the leather bag, the binoculars to its case and refastened the metal grill plate to the wall.

He looked outside. The street was quiet. No police.

His shoulders felt tense. He shrugged, rolled his back, sighed.

He was tired.

A short nap was in order. He would sleep for an hour,

then rent another car from a different company and resume his surveillance of the estate.

Retribution was better accomplished when one was well rested. And if tonight went well, tomorrow would be a very eventful day.

CHAPTER 11

HERNANDO DIAZ WAS STOPPED the second he walked into the rear entrance of the El Carvery meat processing plant. He recognized the man, one of Diego Mendoza's main enforcers, from their previous altercation at the front gate of the orphanage.

"Arms," the man said.

Hernando knew what he meant. He raised his arms. The man patted him down.

"Turn."

Hernando did as he was told, waited for the body search to be concluded.

Satisfied Hernando was not concealing any weapons, the man asked, "What do you want?"

"Diego," Hernando said.

"Mr. Mendoza is not available."

"Tell him to make himself available."

"You don't listen very well," the man said. "What's the message, old man?"

Hernando pointed to the walkie-talkie affixed to the man's belt. "Tell him I'm here. I want to arrange a meeting." He walked to a folding metal chair in the corner beside the receiving door, sat down. "Also tell him if he keeps me waiting I might change my mind."

The man stared at Hernando, then unclipped the walkie-talkie from his belt and walked away. The factory noise muted the conversation. The man returned. "Mr. Mendoza will see you now," he said. "Follow me."

"What a surprise," Hernando replied.

Diego Mendoza sat behind the desk in his second-floor office and motioned to Hernando to enter the room. "Good of you to come by, Mr. Diaz," he said politely.

"You haven't given me much of a choice," Hernando replied.

Mendoza opened his arms, motioned for him to sit. "There are always choices," the drug lord replied. "Whether we make the right one is what counts."

Hernando chose to stand. "And putting my children to work for you is the right choice?"

"From where I sit it is."

"Not to me."

"Then why are you here?"

"To change your mind," Hernando replied.

Mendoza leaned back in his chair. "How do you propose to do that?"

Forget the meeting, Hernando decided. He opened his jacket pocket, removed a thick envelope, tossed it on Diego's desk.

The narco motioned to his bodyguard. The man picked it up, examined its contents, nodded at Diego.

"Fifty-thousand dollars, in cash," Hernando said. "Marcella and I pooled our savings. It's everything we have. Please take it and leave us alone."

Mendoza laughed. "I'm willing to pay you millions

of dollars a year for the use of your children and you offer me a paltry fifty-thousand dollars?" He checked his watch. "I've made that since we've been talking."

"My children are not for sale, Mr. Mendoza."

"Then you've made a grave mistake coming here."

"There is nothing you can do to change my mind," Hernando said. "They will never be for sale."

Diego Mendoza rose from his desk. "Do you realize where you are?"

Hernando said nothing.

The drug lord stepped closer. "Come here," he said. He walked to his office window, looked down on the factory floor. Dozens of employees worked busily at the rendering stations cutting, chopping and sawing meat, preparing it for packaging.

Hernando didn't move. The bodyguard nudged him from behind. He rose and joined Diego at the window.

"This is one of four such factories I own," Diego said. "El Carvery processes enough meat to serve all of Costa Rica. In all the years we've been in business our facilities have never been cited for a health violation or failed a federal inspection. Do you know why that is?"

"Should I care?" Hernando replied.

"It's because I *own* the inspectors, Mr. Diaz. I put money in their pockets, clothes on their children's backs, pools in their backyards, cars in their driveways. It's simple economics. Everyone has a price. Once you know what it is, and you pay it, your problems go away."

"Is there a reason you're telling me this?" Hernando asked.

"Of course," Diego replied. "You are one such problem, Hernando. And I need you to go away."

The blow to the back of Hernando's legs, delivered by the bodyguard, came as if on cue. He fell to his knees, cried out in pain.

Diego stood over the orphanage director, looked down. Hernando tried not to show the immense pain he was feeling, couldn't. His kneecaps felt as though they had shattered on impact with the hard floor. He he was going to be sick to his stomach. He leaned forward, fought back the urge. The gold crucifix he wore around his neck dangled in front of his open jacket. Mendoza grabbed the chain, pulled hard, snapped it off, held it in his hand. "Take him to the freezers," he demanded.

"No!" Hernando cried. He tried impossibly to stand as the bodyguard lifted him to his feet, then collapsed into his arms, his injured legs unable to support the weight of his body.

"My employees have seen it all before," Diego called out as the bodyguard dragged Hernando out of his office towards the flight of stairs. "I own their silence."

Petrified with fear, Hernando screamed, cried out for help.

"Plead all you want, Mr. Diaz," Mendoza yelled. "No one will come to your aid." He returned to his office window and watched as the enforcer manhandled the fragile old man across the processing floor. Around him, Mendoza's employees went about their jobs cutting, trimming and chopping. No one looked up. Hernando's cries fell on deaf ears.

Diego walked to his desk, pressed the intercom button on his telephone. His secretary answered. "Yes, sir?"

"Get me Matias."

"Right away, sir."

Less than a minute later the man knocked on the office door. "You wanted to see me, sir?"

Diego held up the crucifix. "Take this," he said. "Deliver it to the orphanage but do it quietly."

"You want me to send a message?"

"Precisely."

Matias took the necklace from Diego. "Consider it done." He turned to leave.

"One more thing."

"Yes, sir?"

"Assemble a team. We move on the orphanage tonight."

Matias nodded. "As you wish."

∞ ∞ ∞

The black Hummer rolled to a stop in front of the main gate of Casa de los Niños. Matias stepped out of the vehicle, hung the broken necklace on the gate latch, then returned to the car and drove away.

The crucifix turned in the gentle breeze, gleamed in the sunlight.

Message delivered.

CHAPTER 12

JORDAN AND CHRIS presented their credentials to the guard at the main entrance to Joint Forces Training Base Los Alamitos and were immediately directed to DARPA's private jet which awaited them on the tarmac. The agents boarded the aircraft and took their seats.

Chris turned to Jordan. "You sure you're up for this, J?" he asked.

Jordan looked out the window of the aircraft and nodded. "I think so."

"That hardly sounds reassuring," Chris said. "We've seen what Egan can do. There's a good chance this might not end well for either of us. Personally, I'd prefer to hear a little more conviction in your voice than that."

"I can't hide that I'm concerned," Jordan said. "But I'll be damned if I'm not going to try to stop him. Too many people have died because of his actions and those of Dr. Merrick. If I can help to put an end to this, I will."

"Fair enough," Chris said. "No one ever said this job would be easy."

"I know what I signed up for when I joined the bureau and the responsibility that comes with the job," Jordan said. "I'm just glad you've got my back."

"Always," Chris replied.

The co-pilot stepped out of the flight deck and secured the aircraft for takeoff. The Gulfstream's engines whined. He checked on his passengers. "All set agents?" he asked.

"What's the in-flight movie?" Chris asked.

The co-pilot smiled. "Sorry," he said. "This is an entertainment-free flight. U.S military business only."

"Fine," Chris said. "I'll settle for a bag of peanuts."

The co-pilot laughed. "Sorry, no food either. Consider this your tax dollars at work."

Chris turned to Jordan. "Got any food in your purse, J?"

"You're kidding me, right?" Jordan said.

"What? I'm hungry."

"How old are you?" Jordan asked. "Five?"

"Very funny," Chris said. "Flying always gives me the munchies."

Jordan removed a package of breath mints from her purse. She handed him the roll. "Here you go," she said.

Chris looked at the package. "What am I supposed to do with these?" he asked.

"Most people eat them."

"These are candies."

"Use your imagination," Jordan said. "Think of it as a steak dinner without the calories."

"You're cruel," Chris said. He unwrapped the mint, popped it in his mouth.

Jordan smiled. "I'll buy lunch when we land," she said.

"I could be dead by then," Chris replied. "Starvation is a terrible way to go."

"I'm sure you'll survive."

Chris stared at the roll of candies. "Steak dinner, huh?"

"With potatoes and veggies."

"Now you're just being mean."

Jordan smiled. She opened her purse and removed the Chinese puzzle box.

"You brought the needle sheath?" Chris asked.

Jordan nodded. "I need it to connect with the commander, find out where he is."

Jordan removed the needle from the box, held it in her hand and prepared herself for whatever was to come. Seconds later the psychic connection was complete. She found herself back in the tropical region.

"What do you see, Jordan?" Chris asked.

Jordan reported on her surroundings. "Palm trees... a building."

"Do you see the thin man?"

"No."

"What about the children?"

In the dreamlike state, Jordan walked around the compound. "I hear voices," she said. "Children laughing... playing."

"Do you see Commander Egan? Is he there?"

Jordan shook her head. "No."

"What else?" Chris asked.

Jordan looked toward the front gate, walked to it. Above, a sign swung in the gentle breeze. "Casa de los Niños," she said.

"What did you say?" Chris asked.

"The name of the place. It's where I am. Casa de los

Niños."

"That's good," Chris said. "Do you see any other markings? Anything that can tell you where you are geographically?"

"Wait," Jordan said. She heard the rumble of an approaching truck, then watched the vehicle roll past. The company's logo was on the side. She read the name aloud. "Sun Tropic Fresh Fruit Distributors, San Carlos, Costa Rica."

"That's it," Chris said.

Jordan suddenly brought her hands to her head, gripped the needle sheath tighter.

"Are you all right, Jordan?" Chris asked. "What's going on?"

The pain in her head was almost unbearable. "I can feel him," Jordan said.

"You mean Egan?" Chris asked.

Jordan nodded. "He's here."

One hour later the aircraft touched down in Arlington, Virginia. Quentin Hallier and his team were waiting on the tarmac. The jet taxied to a stop. The door opened. Jordan and Chris descended the stairs and greeted the colonel.

Hallier shook hands with the agents. He pointed to the Hercules cargo plane waiting nearby. Its engines whined as it idled. A team of DARPA soldiers, dressed in civilian clothes, were busy loading weapons and gear into the rear hold of the aircraft.

"This plane is our cover," Hallier said, "a long-haul

humanitarian aid flight scheduled to airdrop emergency rations in the Central African Republic. We're catching a ride."

"I have a location where we can find Commander Egan, Colonel," Jordan said. "He's in Costa Rica. A place called 'Casa de los Niños.'"

"You connected with him?" Hallier asked.

"With his energy signature, sir."

"So you didn't *see* him?"

"Not physically, no," Jordan said. "But it's him. I know it is."

Hallier nodded. "That's good enough for me. We'll get an exact location on Casa de los Niños when we're in the air." He pointed to the aircraft. "Stow your gear and grab a seat. We're wheels up in ten minutes."

"Copy that, Colonel," Jordan replied.

Chris accompanied his partner to the plane. "So much for lunch," he said.

Jordan smiled. "Have another mint."

Chris shook his head. "I don't think I can handle two steak dinners in a row."

"I have gum, too," Jordan teased.

"You're a regular gourmet, aren't you?" Chris replied.

CHAPTER 13

ELTON MANNAFORT TOSSED the leather satchel onto the passenger seat of the black GMC Acadia Denali, drove the vehicle out of the rental car parking lot and headed for the Quest estate.

He was certain he was being followed, not by one surveillance vehicle, but by ten. In fact, every vehicle that surrounded him drew his suspicion. He diverted from his intended route and took the interstate ten miles out of his way to shake his pursuers. In a last-ditch attempt to be free of them, he sped along the highway, weaving dangerously in and out of traffic. At the last second, he cut across two lanes and made the exit ramp, nearly rolling the car as he careened around the tight turn. He slammed on the brakes as he reached the stoplight, took a hard right at the corner, then hit the gas. Half a mile down the road he pulled the car into a busy grocery store parking lot, found a spot, killed the engine, and waited.

"You did it."

"You think so?" Elton answered.

"We made it, didn't we?"

Elton was frustrated. "I should have seen them earlier," he replied.

"You're right. Pay closer attention next time."

"I'm trying."

"Not good enough. Try harder."

"There were too many of them."

"You got away, didn't you?"

"Yes."

"Then what are you worried about?"

Elton calmed down. "We should wait here. At least for a few minutes."

"What for?"

"I'd feel better if we did."

"You're not scared, are you?"

"No."

"Sounds like it."

"*I'm not,*" Elton said.

"Prove it. Get back on the road."

"You sure it's safe?"

"You brought the gun?"

"Yes."

"Then what are you worried about? Take it out."

Elton removed the Colt semi-automatic from the satchel.

"Is it ready?"

Elton chambered a round, removed the safety. "Yes."

"Good. Put it in the glove box."

Elton secured the handgun.

"Now leave. You're wasting time."

Elton dropped the Denali into gear, eased out of the parking space and cruised through the lot. He stopped for a young woman, waited for her as she pushed her shopping cart to her car, opened the tailgate and waved thank you. He smiled, waved back. "I like her," he said.

"Forget it. We don't have time."

"Pity," Elton replied.

"Stay focused."

"It wouldn't take long."

"Who's more important, her or the Quest woman?"

"You're right," Elton said.

"You're too easily distracted."

"I'm sorry."

"How far away are we?"

"Thirty minutes."

"We should eat first."

"All right," Elton said. "Denny's?"

"We had pancakes yesterday."

"Red Robin then?"

"A burger sounds good."

Elton reached the street entrance to the grocery store, waited at the intersection for the signal light to turn green and checked out the passing vehicles. He was confident he had evaded the pursuit. "We're good," he said.

With the changing of the light he pulled into traffic and cruised down the road.

"You know what happened wasn't your fault, don't you?"

"I don't want to talk about it," Elton replied nervously.

"You should. They said if you did it would help."

"It doesn't."

"Your parents were to blame, not you."

"I tried to make them understand," Elton said.

"That's all you can do."

"It wasn't enough," Elton answered.

"It never is."

Elton gripped the steering wheel, squeezed it as hard as he could. "She shouldn't have been left alone with me."

"The bitch had it coming."

"That's beside the point." Elton replied. He checked his mirrors. He was not being followed. He opened the satchel, took out the map, unfolded it on the passenger seat, checked his notes. "She'll be picking them up from school soon."

"Are we taking them tonight?"

"Maybe."

"You're not getting cold feet, are you?"

"Of course not," Elton replied.

"Then what's the problem?"

Elton was angry. "Who has more experience with this, you or me?"

"You do."

"That's right. So shut up and let me make the decisions."

"I'm just doing my job."

"What the hell is that supposed to mean?"

"Someone has to keep you on track."

"And I suppose that someone is you?"

"That's right."

Elton scoffed. "If I need your help, I'll ask for it."

"By then it'll probably be too late."

"I'll take my chances."

The traffic slowed. Flashing amber arrows warned of the narrowing lane ahead. Construction crews were setting out orange pylons, waving cars around the broken water main. From the merging lane, a police car fell in behind Elton. He checked his mirror, looked at the cop.

"He knows."

Elton shook his head. "He'd light me up if he did."

"You need to get us out of here."

"And go where? We're in a single lane of traffic."

"That's up to you. Figure it out."

Elton looked at the cop, watched as he turned to his partner and laughed.

"Take out the gun."

"That won't be necessary," Elton replied.

"You really want to take that chance?"

"You're overreacting," Elton said.

"No, I'm not."

"I'm not killing a cop."

"You've developed a conscience all of a sudden?"

"He's not a threat."

"*Yet.*"

"We're safe," Elton said. "We'll be fine just as long as you don't act like an idiot."

"I'm just being careful."

"I know."

"It's my job to watch out for you."

"*I know.*"

Elton cleared the construction zone, continued down

the road. Behind him the police car turned, headed west. "See?" he said. "No threat."

"You got lucky this time."

"It's not luck."

"Oh, I forgot… *experience*."

"That's right," Elton said.

"So, what's the plan?"

"You mean for the family?"

"Yes."

"To make them disappear," Elton replied.

"How do you plan to do that? They're too well-protected."

"Not well enough."

"What do you mean?"

"There's a hole in their security."

"That couldn't have been easy to find."

"It wasn't."

"And after?"

"After what?"

"After you've taken care of the family."

Alone in the car, Elton spoke to the empty seat beside him. "Then I kill the woman."

CHAPTER 14

THE PSYCHIC CONNECTION struck Ben Egan with such force he turned away from his work mending the fence to see who was standing behind him. He was certain he was not alone, yet he was. He had felt this level of intrusion before, this uncanny mind-meld to his superior, artificially enhanced brain.

The FBI agent.

Her energy was much stronger this time. During their last encounter, when she had tracked him and found him on the jungle trail after the completion of his mission, he had warned her not to follow him. She had seen the unparalleled power of Channeler, just days ago at the University when he had caused the Pyramid to fall. She knew what he was capable of.

There was no way she would attempt to challenge him on her own. Which meant only one thing.

They were coming for him.

He tried to reach out, connect with the woman, couldn't. She was gone.

There was only one option now. He would soon have to be on the move again. Eventually the DARPA commandos would find him. When that time came, he couldn't afford to have Hernando, Marcella, or the children caught in the line of fire. The assault would go down hard and fast, the soldiers following capture-kill orders. He well knew his immense military value and that he was a top-secret asset in need of termination.

Not going to happen.

As far as he was concerned, he had already served his purpose for the military. He had accepted the challenge of Project Genesis and proven it to be an unparalleled success. DARPA had responded by trying to kill him and succeeded in taking the life of his handler, Dr. Jason Merrick.

This was a no-win situation if ever there was one. If he was to survive, he would have to gain the upper hand and fight back harder than ever before.

From across the compound, Marcella screamed.

Egan dropped the hammer and ran to the gate.

In her hand, Marcella held Hernando's necklace. She stared at the dangling crucifix.

Marcella looked at Egan. "They have him," she cried.

Egan took the necklace from her hand, concentrated, saw the meat-processing facility, the freezer. Marcella watched his hand glow. The crucifix reflected the unnatural energy, glimmered rose-red. Unaware of the extent of his strange and miraculous powers, she asked, "What do you see?"

"He's hurt."

"Oh, God."

"There are many people around him," Egan said. "It appears to be a manufacturing facility of some kind. Does that mean anything to you?"

"It could be Le Carvery."

"What's that?"

"One of Diego Mendoza's businesses. It supplies meat to most of the food stores and restaurants in the country."

"How far is it from here?"

"Forty-five minutes."

Egan handed her the necklace. He looked down the road. They were not being watched. He turned to Marcella. "Get the children ready to leave."

"Why?"

"They're what Mendoza really wants," Egan said. "Them, and the orphanage. He doesn't care about Hernando."

Marcella covered her mouth in horror. The words came hard. "He's going to kill him, isn't he?" she asked.

"I won't give him that chance," Egan replied.

"What are you going to do?"

"Find Diego."

"And then?"

"Give him the proper incentive to release Hernando."

"You won't get close to him," Marcella warned. "He has an army of men to protect him."

"He'll need one," Egan said. "How soon can you have the kids ready to go?"

"Half an hour," Marcella said.

"Good," Egan said. "I'll need wheels."

"Take mine," Marcella said. She pointed to a Hyundai Accent parked outside the entrance to the office. "It's not much to look at but it runs."

"Works for me," Egan replied. "Where do I find Le

Carvery?"

Marcella handed him her keys. "My car has a GPS," she said. "I'll enter the address. Follow the route. It'll take you there."

Egan nodded. "Thanks."

Marcella took his hand. "Before you leave, there's something I need to ask you, Ben."

Egan paused, waited for the question.

"Why are you doing this?" Marcella asked. "You don't know us. You have no cause in this fight. You could just turn and walk away. No one would blame you if you did. Yet here you are."

"I have a very low tolerance for men like Diego Mendoza who prey on the weak," Egan replied. "I can't stand by and watch this happen. It's not in my nature. Besides, these children need you and Hernando. I won't let him destroy their future or yours."

Marcella smiled. "First you save Teresa's life, now we might owe you ours," she said.

Egan patted her hand. "I know I'm asking you to put a lot of trust in me, Marcella. Believe me when I say everything will be all right. But there's something you need to prepare yourself for."

"What's that?"

"Things are going to get worse before they get better. Maybe a lot worse."

"I figured as much," Marcella said.

"You mentioned there was a church that was willing to take the children," Egan said.

"Yes," Marcella replied. "In San Jose. St. Jude's."

"Take the van and get the children as far away from here as you can," Egan said. "Go to the church. I'll get word to you when this is over. You and the children can return then, but not before."

"I'm scared, Ben," Marcella said. "What if something happens to you and Hernando?"

"Don't worry, we'll be fine," Egan answered.

"You can't be sure of that."

"You just take care of the children," Egan insisted. "Leave the rest to me."

CHAPTER 15

FOUR HOURS AFTER LEAVING Arlington the DARPA pilot made an announcement. "We're entering Costa Rican airspace, Colonel," he said. "Five minutes to exit point."

"Copy that," Hallier replied. To his men he said, "Gear up. Check your three's."

The soldiers donned their parachutes and jumpsuits, checked their harness attachments and operational handle positions. Secure.

Hallier handed Jordan and Chris their jumpsuits and parachutes.

Jordan slipped into the garment and put on the chute.

Chris held the items in his hand. "What exactly am I supposed to do with these?" he asked.

"I'd suggest you put them on," Jordan replied.

"No one said anything about jumping out of an airplane!" Chris exclaimed.

"Life is full of surprises."

"I've never parachuted in my life," Chris said. "Shouldn't we have taken lessons first?"

"What's to learn?" Jordan replied. "You jump, wait a few seconds, hit minimum altitude, then float to the ground."

Chris stared at her. "Minimum altitude?" he said. "I'd prefer *maximum* altitude. Actually, I'd prefer no altitude at all!"

"Don't be a baby," Jordan replied.

"What if my chute doesn't open?" Chris asked.

"Don't worry, it will," Jordan said. "It has a fail-safe device that will ensure it opens."

"But what if it *doesn't*?"

Jordan smiled. "Then I'll be sure to feed J. Edgar."

"Nice of you to bring my goldfish into it," Chris replied.

"Really, Chris," Jordan said. "Parachuting is no big deal."

"Let me guess. You've done this before?"

"Many times."

"Is there a trick to it?"

"Absolutely."

"Now would be a good time to share."

Jordan smiled. "Don't look down."

"Excuse me?" Chris said. He reluctantly slipped into the jumpsuit, donned the parachute.

Jordan adjusted his harness and handles. "There's really nothing to be afraid of," she said. "When you reach altitude, your chute will automatically deploy."

"I have a better idea," Chris offered. "What do you say we put this baby on the ground, with me in it, all safe and sound. I'll grab a bus and catch up with you later."

Jordan motioned to the armed DARPA commandos standing in line, waiting for the Hercules' rear cargo door to open. "The Costa Rican government prefers visitors not bring fully automatic weapons and other restricted ordinance onto their buses. It tends to make people nervous," she said.

"To be fair," Chris said, "they also don't expect visitors to enter their country by jumping out of an airplane."

"This is an off-the-books operation, remember?" Jordan replied.

"The least they could do is have a free rum punch waiting for us when we land," Chris said.

"One minute to DZ," the pilot announced. The rear door of the cargo plane began to open.

"Put these on," Jordan said. She handed Chris a pair of goggles. "And keep your mouth closed. Breathe through your nose."

"Of course," Chris replied. "Because when I'm falling through the air at a million miles an hour my only concern will be the wind ripping my face off."

"Actually, we probably won't be falling any faster than one-hundred-and-thirty miles per hour."

"*One-hundred-and-thirty*," Chris repeated. "How comforting."

"Remember," Jordan said. "Close your mouth. I'd hate to see you ruin that perfect smile of yours."

The pilot spoke. "Thirty seconds to drop zone."

The cargo door locked open. The outside wind rushed into the aircraft. The soldiers readied themselves for the jump. Jordan and Chris took their place at the back of the cue.

"We'll jump together," Jordan said. "Keep your eyes on me." The agents shuffle-stepped to the rear of the plane. "Do what I do and you'll be fine."

"And if I don't?" Chris replied.

"I have a dog," Jordan said. "I really don't need a goldfish too."

"Very funny."

"Ten seconds," the pilot announced.

Jordan provided last-minute instructions. "When you jump, dive headlong out of the plane. When you do, you're probably going to feel a bump."

"A *bump?*" Chris asked.

"A severe upward push of air caused by turbulence from the planes backwash."

"I have absolutely no clue what you just said. I'm still processing bump."

"Doesn't matter," Jordan said. "Just hope you don't hit an air pocket. If you do, you'll lose altitude in seconds and drop like a rock."

"That's it," Chris said. "I am *not* doing this."

"Ready?" Jordan asked.

Chris yelled above the wind. "Hell, no!"

"Five… four…"

"On my mark," Jordan said.

"Three… two…"

"*Mark?* Chris yelled. "What mark?"

"Go! Go! Go!" the pilot called out.

Jordan grabbed Chris by his harness and threw herself, and him, out of the Hercules. Together they fell through the sky… down… down… down.

Jordan watched as Chris' parachute deployed and carried the agent back up into the air. Slowly, he began to descend. Jordan maneuvered her parachute steering lines and floated towards Chris. Chris watched, followed her directions. As they approached the ground, Jordan pulled down hard on her steering lines, as did Chris, and braked her landing. The agents touched down featherlight onto the ground. Around them, already landed, the team of DARPA commandos were busy storing their chutes.

Jordan walked over to Chris. "You okay?" she asked.

Chris' face was white. He raised his hand. "Never ask me to do that again," he replied.

Jordan smiled. "Oh, come on. It wasn't that bad."

Chris shook his head disapprovingly. "Not for you, maybe. Personally, I think I peed a little."

Hallier walked across the drop zone, joined the agents. "Nice jump," he said. "You both looked pretty comfortable up there."

"Piece of cake, Colonel," Chris replied nonchalantly. He gave Hallier the thumbs up. "We should do it again sometime."

Jordan shot him a furtive glance. Chris winked.

A large panel truck rolled up to the edge of the drop zone and flashed its lights. Hallier waved.

Jordan pointed to the truck. "Looks like our ride is here," she said.

In the sky above, the drone of the Hercules' engines faded as it continued onward toward its final destination.

On the ground, the search for Ben Egan had begun.

CHAPTER 16

HERNANDO TRACED THE FROST-COVERED walk-in freezer walls with his fingertips, searched for the light switch located beside the door, found it, flipped it on. Overhead, the lighting fixture flickered, flashed to life, and bathed the room in harsh white light. Dozens of boxes of processed meat products surrounded him, stacked high on wooden pallets, ready for shipment to El Carvery's customers. He located the cold rooms emergency door release, installed to provide a means of escape should the door accidentally close and lock behind an inattentive worker, pushed hard against the plunger knob, then tried to turn the lever. The device wouldn't budge. On closer inspection Hernando saw that the mechanism had been tampered with, rendering it useless. He was trapped in the bitter cold room. Red numbers glared at him from an LED display integrated into the wall beside the door handle: -40 degrees. Though he had been in the freezer for less than ten minutes, he knew his chances for survival under such conditions was slim. In the sub-zero temperature his body was already losing heat at an alarming rate. Hernando rubbed his arms and legs vigorously, trying to promote the circulation of blood within his limbs and keep himself warm. It wouldn't be long before hypothermia would set in, followed by the functional breakdown of his brain, heart and internal organs. Already his skin had begun to tighten. He had lost sensation in his fingertips, ears and toes. He was having difficulty breathing now, and the numbness and tingling he was experiencing throughout the rest of his body, coupled with an odd burning sensation, warned that death from continued exposure to the extreme cold was imminent. His clothing –jeans, a light jacket, cotton golf shirt, socks and running shoes- though appropriate for the tropical Costa Rican climate, offered no protection against the arctic cold temperature of the freezer.

Hernando kicked at the heavy freezer door. Strangely, he could not feel the impact. His foot was numb. He swung the useless extremity at the door a second time… *thump*… then a third. Exhausted after the weak attempt to be heard, he leaned against a pallet of boxed, frozen meat. His mind began to wander to Marcella and the children. He worried about their safety. Had Diego Mendoza already sent his men to take over the orphanage in his absence? Had they already put the children to work packaging his drugs? He couldn't let that happen, *wouldn't* let that happen.

Hernando summoned what strength remained in his shaking, cold-beaten body and screamed as loud and long as he could.

A moment of silence followed, then the sound of movement outside the freezer door.

Whoosh.

Hernando felt the incoming rush of warm air as the door opened. Diego Mendoza stood in the doorway. The drug lord addressed him. "Have you come to your senses, Mr. Diaz?" he said.

Hernando simply stared at his captor. He shook uncontrollably. He tried to reply but the words wouldn't come, his ability to speak rendered impossible from prolonged exposure to the bitter cold of the freezer.

Mendoza instructed his men. "Take him to the storeroom. Give him a blanket and a cup of hot coffee. When he has warmed up enough to talk, call me. And don't let him out of your sight."

"Yes, sir," the men replied.

Hernando had lost all sensation in his legs and feet. He struggled to stand as the men extricated him from the freezer. Walking had become impossible. He fell into their arms.

In the storeroom, wrapped in a heavy shipping blanket, Hernando tried to raise the cup of steaming hot coffee to his lips but couldn't. His hands were shaking so violently that he dropped the mug. It shattered on the concrete floor. His only option was to wait until the heat returned to his body.

"Hurry and heat up, old man," one enforcer said as he picked up the broken pieces of the coffee mug off the floor. "Mr. Mendoza won't wait forever."

Hernando struggled to reply. "He'll… w-wait… f-for me."

The men laughed. "You think so?"

Hernando's head quivered as he nodded. He forced a smile. "Know… s-so."

"You seem pretty sure of yourself," one of the thugs answered.

"I am," Hernando said. He massaged his arms and legs. He could feel the heat returning to his body.

One of the enforcers took Hernando by the arm, helped him up from the chair. "Get up," he said. "You're fine now."

"Still c-cold," Hernando replied. He fell back into the chair.

"You'll survive," the man said.

Hernando spied a heavy parka used by Le Carvery's freezer workers hanging from a hook on the wall of the storeroom. He pointed to it. "P-please," he said.

"You want the coat?" the man asked.

Hernando nodded. "W-warmer," he said.

The thug checked with his partner and shrugged. "What could it hurt?" he asked.

The enforcer agreed, nodded. "Give him the damn coat."

Hernando dropped the shipping blanket to the floor and slipped into the heavy jacket. He shivered. "B-better," he said. "Thank you."

"Whatever gets your ass out of here the fastest," the enforcer replied.

Hernando shoved his hands deep into the front pockets of the jacket, pulled it tight around him, felt an object in the right pocket, and immediately recognized it by its shape and feel. His stomach turned at the thought of what he was about to do.

The pot of coffee sat on the burner in the storeroom.

Hernando pointed to it. "Can I h-have another c-cup?" he asked.

"You gonna drop this one too?" the enforcer asked.

"No," Hernando answered. "Please?"

The man looked at his partner. "This is like taking care of a fucking child," he complained. To Hernando he said, "All right. Have your coffee. Then we see the boss. And you better be ready to tell him exactly what he wants to hear."

Hernando nodded.

The enforcer turned to pour the coffee.

In an instant, Hernando pulled the box cutter out of the pocket of the parka, opened the blade and struck out. He grabbed the enforcer from behind, pulled his head back and slit his throat. Dumbfounded at the speed of Hernando's instantaneous attack, the man's partner attempted to draw his gun from his waistband. Too late, Hernando slashed the thug's face with the blade. The man dropped the weapon as he tried to stop the flow of blood pouring from the laceration. Hernando picked up the gun, forced the man back against the storeroom wall, drove the barrel deep into his belly, then fired twice. The dense material of the heavy winter parka muffled the sound of the gunshots. Hernando watched the dead man's hand fall away from his face as he lowered the body to the floor.

It was over.

Hernando removed the heavy parka, tossed it on the chair, and slipped the box cutter into his pocket. He shoved the gun into his waistband and covered it with his shirt.

Slowly, he cracked open the door to the storeroom and peered outside. All quiet. No one had heard the shots. He could hear no voices in the vicinity.

Hernando stepped out of the room, closed the door behind him, walked to the corner and inspected the area. The storeroom was located in a dark and quiet section of the warehouse, far away from the factory workers and the meat production floor. He wondered how many others before him had been held in that room and tortured or killed at Diego Mendoza's command.

Ahead, sunlight poured in through a dusty window above an exit door.

Hernando opened it, found freedom and ran.

CHAPTER 17

THE CROWN VICTORIA SEDAN Elton Mannafort wanted could not be found at any of the car rental companies he approached, so he did the next best thing: he turned to the Internet. A private seller on a used car buy-and-sell website was selling the exact make and model he was looking for. Elton visited the seller's country home, learned the old fellow had been an avid collector of used police vehicles for the past ten years, and carefully inspected each of the six vehicles he kept in his barn. Four of the sedans were being sold for parts, leaving two available for sale. Elton settled on a pristine eight-year-old dark gray model, complete with a door-mounted searchlight which the driver could operate from inside the vehicle. This unmarked squad car was extra special. Its emergency service lights and siren were still intact, hidden behind the front grill of the car.

The old man started the Crown Vic, turned on the service lights and side-door searchlight, and blared the siren for a few seconds. "Everything works perfectly," he told Elton. "She runs like a charm. Interior's in beautiful shape too." He exited the car and held the door open for Elton. "Hop in. Check it out for yourself."

Elton sat behind the wheel. The old man was right. The vehicle was in immaculate condition.

"Federal law says private citizens can't operate the

lights and siren," the man pointed out. "Actually, the car is not allowed to be sold with them, but I got lucky. I inherited it from the widow of a buddy who was an ex-cop. We'd been working together to restore it. One day I got a call from his wife telling me he'd passed away. Massive heart attack. Dropped dead on the spot, poor bastard. She figured he would have wanted me to have the car. Can't say as I really want to sell it, though. I've got a lot of fond memories tied up in this old girl. Why do you want it?"

"I'm a Hollywood acquisitions manager," Elton lied. "I find props for the movie industry. My client is shooting a film. He needs a working Crown Victoria, just like this one."

"The movies, huh?" the old man said. "Just how big is your budget?"

Elton smiled. "Your ad said you wanted seven grand for the car, so seven grand it is."

The man stroked his chin. "I don't know," he replied thoughtfully. "I might just keep her. You know, sentimental value and all."

"How sentimental would you feel if I raised the offer to eight thousand?" Elton said.

The old man ran his hand across the roof of the car. "She's still plucking at my heartstrings."

"Would ten grand end the relationship?" Elton asked. He removed an envelope from his pocket and flashed the bills. "Cash money."

The old man smiled, held out his hand. "I'm breaking up with her already," he said.

Elton handed him the money. "I thought you might."

The old man counted the cash. "Happy?" Elton asked.

"Very." The man offered his hand to seal the deal.

"I'll be taking it now," Elton said.

"You gonna have it towed?"

Elton shook his head. "No, I'll drive it now."

The old man looked puzzled. He glanced at Elton's car parked in the driveway. "What about your car?" he asked.

"I don't need it anymore," Elton replied. "Would you mind if I parked it in here?"

"What are you talking about, mister?" the old man said. "I can't let you park your car…"

Elton stepped out of the car, removed his gun from his waistband and placed it against the old man's forehead.

"Oh, God!" the man cried. He offered Elton the cash-filled envelope. "Here, take it. And the car. Just don't kill me."

"Too late," Elton replied.

"No!"

"You've seen my face."

"Please…" the old man begged. He dropped to his knees.

"Who else is in the house?"

"No one," the man replied.

"You live alone?"

The old man nodded.

"Good," Elton said. "Nothing personal." He pulled

the trigger. The gunshot echoed off the walls of the barn. The old man fell to his side. Elton dragged the corpse to one of the parts cars, deposited the body into the trunk and closed the lid.

The old man could have been lying, protecting his spouse or a child, perhaps. Elton strolled from the barn to the house, entered the property through the back door and searched every room. Clear. The man had been telling the truth.

Elton parked the rental car into the spacious barn, drove out the Crown Victoria, then rolled shut the heavy barn door. He knew the rental company had equipped the vehicle with an anti-theft GPS tracking system. Eventually it would be located. No matter. The identification he had used to rent the vehicle had been fake. The mustache, goatee and glasses he had worn were sufficient a disguise to hide his face from the rental company's security cameras. He had even completed the paperwork using his left hand, although he was right-handed; more theater for the benefit of the security cameras. By the time the vehicle was flagged as being well past its required return date and its last known position reported to the company, he would be long gone. His physical description would be useless to the authorities.

"Now what?" he said aloud.

He checked his watch. Three P.M.

"The housekeeper will be picking up the children soon."

"Relax, there's plenty of time."

"Don't be so cocky."

"I'm not. I know her schedule, remember?"

"So, is today the day?"

"I don't see any reason why not."

"You sure you're ready for this?"

"They'll never see it coming."

"There you go again."

"What?"

"Being cocky."

"It's called confidence."

"You know you'll have to take out the security detail."

"Do I sound like I'm worried about that?"

"Perhaps you should be."

"I'm not."

"Prove it."

Elton slowly drove the used police car down the driveway and left the old man's property. He turned onto the county road. "I intend to."

CHAPTER 18

THE VOCAL COMMANDS ANNOUNCED by the GPS in Marcella Herrara's car took Ben Egan straight to Le Carvery. He parked the Honda Accord across the street from the massive meat processing facility, held Hernando's necklace in his hand, closed his eyes and concentrated.

The man's energy signal was crystal clear. He could feel his presence. He was close.

Egan exited the vehicle and walked along the side of the road. At the rear of the plant, tractor trailers were parked in loading bays. He could hear forklifts as they drove their cargo into the holds of the trucks and dropped each heavy pallet into place. Deep inside the factory, cutting equipment whined, buzzed and chopped.

Egan passed the loading bays, rounded the corner of the building and spotted Hernando's car parked at the rear entrance. A metal sign on the wall read Employees Only.

He climbed the metal stairs and placed his hand against the door. The reading from the residual energy was strong. Hernando had been here.

Egan cracked opened the door. A folding metal chair stood on the floor to his left. To his right, a staircase led up to the second floor. The area was quiet, unoccupied.

He walked past an employee punch card time clock mounted on the wall at the foot of the stairs and looked around the corner. He could see the main factory floor. Dozens of employees dressed entirely in white, from the disposable hairnets on their heads to the cotton slipcovers worn over their shoes, were at work at their stations. The factory floor was so clean it gleamed. This was as far as he dared to go. Beyond this point he would be at risk of being seen. One employee would surely stop him and ask what he was doing walking about in a restricted area of the factory. That was a problem he did not need. His priority was to find Hernando.

As Egan doubled back to the employee entrance a voice called out to him. He looked up. A man stood at the top of the second-floor staircase. He recognized him immediately as one of Diego Mendoza's enforcers and one of the men he had warned away from the front gates of the orphanage.

"You!" the man called out. As he descended the stairs, he unclipped a walkie-talkie from his belt, spoke into the microphone. From a distance, along the metal catwalk, Egan heard running footfalls. The man had called for backup. Others were coming to his aid.

Egan placed his hand on the steel railing, concentrated and tapped in to his superhuman abilities. The staircase suddenly began to rattle and shake. The man tried to grab hold of the railing, couldn't, lost his balance and fell. He toppled down the stairs and landed hard at Egan's feet. The impact with the floor knocked him unconscious.

The man's backup had finally reached the top of the staircase. The two enforcers looked down at Egan, saw their partner laid out on the ground and drew their weapons.

Egan reassessed the situation. This was not the time or place for a showdown with Mendoza or his men. His first priority was finding Hernando and returning him safely to the orphanage. He would deal with the drug lord later.

The employee entrance was immediately behind him. Egan turned, threw open the door, slammed it shut behind him and placed his palm on the handle. Under the rose-red glow of the mysterious force that was his special gift Egan caused the metal lock assembly to melt into the doorframe, sealing off the exit. From inside the factory he heard the men as they pushed and kicked at the door, trying impossibly to open it. Egan ran around the corner of the factory past the transport trailers and along the roadway. He didn't stop until he reached Marcella's car. Suddenly a voice called out his name. "Ben?"

Egan wheeled around.

Across the street, Hernando Diaz stepped out from behind the parked car where he had been hiding. "What are you doing here?" he asked.

"What do you think?" Egan replied. "Looking for you."

"I told you before," Hernando said defiantly, "this is not your fight."

"Maybe not," Egan answered, "but it's too late now.

I'm invested in you and the kids. And like it or not, you're going to need my help."

"What makes you think so?"

Egan stared at his friend. "I don't see any cuts or scratches, so I'm guessing the blood on your face and hands isn't your own."

Hernando paused, then spoke. "No, it isn't. I didn't have a choice in the matter."

"I know," Egan replied.

Hernando looked surprised. "What do you mean?" he asked.

"Because men like you don't go looking for trouble, Hernando. You would have needed a damn good reason to fight back."

"They tried to kill me."

"And?"

Hernando removed the box cutter from his jeans and showed it to Egan. "I killed them instead."

Egan took the tool from Hernando and put it in his pocket. "We need to get out of here. Now." He opened the car door. "Get in."

Egan started the car, put it into gear, pulled a U-turn, and sped down the road. He looked out the window as he drove past the front entrance to Le Carvery. He watched as the two enforcers burst through the front doors and ran out of the building. One man veered left, the other right. No doubt they were searching for him.

Hernando saw the commotion. "What happened back there?" he asked.

"I ran into a little trouble," Egan replied.

NINE LIVES

"Anybody get hurt?"

"No," Egan said. "But Mendoza will probably have to order a new back door. Probably a new staircase too."

"I'm not following you," Hernando replied.

"Don't worry about it. It's all good."

Hernando dropped his head. "I killed two of Mendoza's men today, Ben," he said. "I didn't even think about it. I just did it." The tone of the admission weighed heavily in his voice. "How am I supposed to live with that?"

Ben glanced at his friend. Hernando's hands were shaking. "Everything's going to be fine, Hernando," he said. "Don't believe for a minute that those men died a death any less violent than what they'd likely inflicted on others. You know what they say."

"What's that?" Hernando asked.

"Karma's a bitch."

"It doesn't change the reality of the situation," Hernando said.

"Like hell it doesn't."

"What do you mean?"

"You're alive," Egan said. "Which means Marcella and the children still have you. In my book that makes all the difference in the world. The world won't miss a couple of dirtbags, but it would sure as hell miss you."

"Thank you, Ben," Hernando replied.

"You're welcome."

Hernando stared out the car window. "They'll come looking for us," he said. "We're all in danger now."

Egan nodded. "I know."

CHAPTER 19

THE DARPA OPERATIVES loaded their weapons and gear into the back of the panel truck and climbed aboard.

The vehicle rocked from side to side as it traveled along the broken back road. Hallier turned to Jordan. "You've taken us halfway around the world, Agent Quest," he said. "Where's Commander Egan?"

Jordan removed the plastic needle sheath from her pocket, closed her eyes and focused on the super-soldier's energy signature. The connection was strong but the location difficult to discern. "I can't say for certain," Jordan replied. "But he *is* here."

Hallier was upset. "Costa Rica is a damn big country," he quipped. "You'll have to do a hell of a lot better than that."

Jordan focused. "He's on the move," she replied. "Which is what's making it difficult to track him to a specific area."

To Jordan, Chris said, "You'd mentioned Egan had a connection to a particular place. Do you remember what it was called?"

Jordan nodded. "Casa de los Niños."

Chris took out his cellphone, searched the name. "Casa de los Niños is an orphanage in La Fortuna," he said. "We're about an hour away."

"Is that where he's headed?" Hallier asked.

"I'm getting a very strong connection between the commander and the orphanage," Jordan replied. "We should check it out."

Hallier nodded. "Very well," he said. He slid open the dividing window between the cab and the rear of the truck and spoke to the driver. "Take us to La Fortuna."

"Copy that, sir," the soldier replied.

Jordan turned to Hallier. "What happens when we find him, Colonel?"

"That will be up to the commander," Hallier replied. "He can come with us quietly or not."

"And if he doesn't?" Jordan asked.

Hallier pointed to a canvas bag laying at his feet. "Then we'll deal with him accordingly."

"What's in the bag?" Chris asked.

"Countermeasures," Hallier replied.

"How can you possibly stop him?" Chris pressed. "The man has the ability to teleport anywhere in the world, at will. How do you deal with someone like that?"

"We wouldn't be here if we couldn't," Hallier replied. "Make no mistake about it. My men are prepared to take whatever action is necessary to end this."

"Agent Quest and I both saw what the commander and Dr. Merrick did to the university in Long Beach," Chris replied. "They decimated the place. Your men didn't stand a chance. Neither did L.A.P.D. SWAT. What's to say that won't happen again?"

"All you need to know is that we're better equipped

to deal with the commander now than we were then," Hallier said.

Suddenly the driver called out. "Colonel, we have a problem."

"What is it?" Hallier asked.

"We've picked up a tail."

"How long have they been following us?" Hallier asked.

"Since we left the drop zone. Probably saw your men parachute in."

"Military?"

"No, sir."

"Police?"

"I don't think so, sir."

"Whoever they are, lose them."

"Yes, sir," the driver replied.

The commando seated beside Hallier spoke. "I've got this, sir." He opened one of the weapons cases and pulled out a gray metal box. It contained a dozen spiked steel balls, each no bigger than a golf ball. "Get some distance between us and the car," he told the driver, "then take the next turn hard and fast."

"Copy that," the driver replied. "Brace yourselves."

The truck increased its speed, raced down the road. The driver spied a secondary route ahead. "Coming up in five… four… three… two… BRACE!"

The commando threw open the rear cargo door and spilled the box of metal caltrops onto the road just as the team's truck made a hard right. The tires of the pursuing vehicle blew out. *Pop! Pop! Pop! Pop!*

Strips of shredded rubber from the cars exploding tires launched into the air then fell to the ground. Smoke and sparks filled the air as it continued down the main road, its steel rims screeching loudly against the pavement.

The driver reported to Hallier. "No secondary vehicles, sir. We're clear."

"Good work," the colonel said. "Get us back on the main road as soon as you can."

"Copy that."

CHAPTER 20

ELTON MANNAFORT PARKED the Crown Victoria police sedan across the street from Benroyal Academy and observed Marissa DeSola as she waited to pick up the Quest children from school. In the student drop-off and pickup area, an operative from the shadow security detail stood vigilant outside the black SUV, keeping the woman's car in sight, while his partner remained seated behind the wheel.

The ring of a bell announced the end of the school day. Elton watched as the front doors burst open and the students began to pour out of the building. Aiden and Emma soon emerged from the boisterous crowd, stopped briefly to chat with their friends, then said their goodbyes. Only after the children had greeted the housekeeper and were safely inside the vehicle did the operative rejoin his partner in the SUV.

Elton removed a silencer from the satchel on the passenger seat beside him and attached it to his handgun. He tucked the weapon under the bag, out of sight. Slowly, the black SUV pulled away from the curb. He watched it follow Marissa and the children as they left the school.

It was time.

Elton cranked the wheel of the sedan hard to the left, executed a fast U-turn, then merged with the traffic flow, careful to maintain a generous following distance behind the protection detail. As the vehicles weaved in and out of traffic, he closed the gap. Several lane changes later he had positioned himself directly behind the SUV.

Marissa's vehicle stopped ahead of the security detail, then executed a right turn at the intersection. The SUV followed her around the corner. Elton sped up. When the vehicle had completed its turn, Elton turned on the unmarked police sedan's service lights and hit the siren.

Slowly, the black SUV pulled over to the curb and braked to a stop.

Elton grabbed the weapon from under the bag, placed it behind his leg, opened the door, exited the vehicle and approached the driver. The driver's window lowered. Elton reached the car and addressed the occupants. "Afternoon," Elton said. "License and registration, please."

The operative removed his sunglasses. "Mind telling me why you're stopping us?" the man asked.

"Failure to stop," Elton replied.

The driver looked puzzled. "Come again?" he asked.

Elton pointed back down the street. "The corner back there. You blew through a four-way stop. Not a good idea to do that in front of the police."

By now Marissa was half a block down the road. Elton knew her schedule for the day. If he didn't catch up to her soon his window of opportunity would be lost.

The driver motioned to his partner. Elton watched as

the man opened the glove box and produced the requested documentation.

The driver removed his credentials from his jacket pocket and presented them to Elton. "We're both on the job, so to speak," the man said. "That's our client we were following. Any chance you could cut us a break, officer?"

"It's *detective*," Elton lied. He read aloud the mans private security identification. "James Holtzman, Sentinel Executive Protection." He looked at the passenger. "And you are?" he asked.

"Jeremy Bennett," the partner replied. He presented his credentials. Elton examined the identification card.

"Who's the client?" Elton asked.

"A VIP," the driver replied.

"Anyone I might know?"

"Maybe. Jordan Quest."

"The psychic?"

The driver nodded. "The same," he replied. "Our firm has been retained to protect the family."

Elton pocketed the men's credentials. "Sounds like a pretty cushy gig," he said.

The driver glanced uncomfortably at his partner then back at Elton. "We'll need those back, detective."

"What's it like working in private security, anyway?" Elton asked. "You guys ever run into any serious trouble?"

The driver shook his head. "Not as a rule," he replied. Elton noticed the change in the driver's demeanor. Holtzman lowered his hands from the steering wheel, placed them in his lap. He had become suspicious. "Sir," he said. "Our ID's."

Bennett too shifted uncomfortably in his seat, then placed his hand on the door handle.

"I've thought about it myself from time to time," Elton replied. "LAPD's can be a drag. Too many rules."

Holtzman casually slipped his hand under his jacket, felt for his weapon in its cross-draw holster, grabbed hold of the gun, held it tight. He smiled at Elton. "I hear you," he said. "Tell you what. Give me your card. Call me when you're ready to leave the force. I'm sure we can find room for you at Sentinel, Detective…"

"Mannafort," Elton replied. "Elton Mannafort."

"Mannafort," Holtzman repeated thoughtfully. Unseen, the operative had drawn his gun from his holster. He held it against his side. "What division?" he asked.

Elton read the body language of the two men. Holtzman's stare was fixed. He knew something was wrong. His fight-or-flight response had kicked in.

Elton glanced left, then right, checked the street. Empty. "Homicide," he replied. He raised the gun and fired. *Thwup… thwup… thwup… thwup.* The four rounds found their respective marks. Holtzman took two to the heart, Bennett to the head. The men slumped forward, dead.

Elton removed a handkerchief from his jacket pocket. He opened the door, closed the driver's window, turned off the car, closed the door and walked back to the Crown Victoria.

Dealing with the shadow security detail had taken longer than he had planned. He checked the clock on the dashboard. By his estimation the housekeeper and the children were only ten minutes from home. He was now several precious minutes behind schedule. He needed to intercept them before they arrived at the estate.

As Elton pulled away from the curb he glanced at the SUV. The heavily tinted windows made it virtually impossible to see inside the vehicle.

The operative's bodies would eventually be found. By then it would be too late. The housekeeper and the children would be dead.

He needed to make up for lost time.

Elton turned on the sedan's siren and sped down the road. Ahead, motorists gave way to the oncoming police car.

CHAPTER 21

EGAN EASED THE CAR to a stop as he reached the front gate of the orphanage. "Something's wrong," he said.

"What's the problem?" Hernando asked.

He pointed to the van parked outside the main office. "Marcella was to have taken the children and left for St. Jude's in San Jose," he said. "The van's still here."

Hernando stared at the compound. "You don't think Mendoza's men have been here already, do you?"

Egan opened the car door, closed it quietly. "Let's hope not."

Hernando stepped out of the vehicle. "Marcella would never let them kidnap the children," he said. "She'd die first."

"Wait here," Egan said. "Let me check it out."

Hernando shook his head. "Not a chance, he replied. "I'm coming with you."

"All right," Egan said. "But stay close. And if I tell you to run, *run*."

"You speak like you've done this before."

"Too many times to count. You ready?"

"Ready."

"Keep low and stay on my six. Follow the perimeter."

"Got it."

"One more thing."

"What's that?"

"If the shit hits the fan, stay down. Let me deal with it."

Hernando hesitated.

Egan stared at the old man. "I mean it, Hernando. I'm trained to handle these situations. You're not. Got it?"

Hernando nodded.

"Good. Let's go."

The men ran into the compound and followed the rickety wooden fence line until they reached the back of the main building. The yard was eerily quiet.

Hernando pressed his ear against the back wall and listened. "I don't hear a thing," he whispered. "Not a sound."

The building was silent. "I'm going around." Egan whispered. "Wait here."

Hernando nodded.

Egan crept around the building, reached the front door, turned the knob.

Locked.

He peered through the front window into the dark room. The building appeared to be empty.

From within the structure he heard a sound, weak yet distinct; a child coughed.

Egan called out. "Marcella? Are you in there? It's me, Ben."

Footsteps, running across the wooden floor. The door locks disengaged. Marcella threw open the door. "Ben!" she cried. "You're safe! Thank God!"

Hernando peered around the corner of the building. Egan looked at the old man, smiled, shook his head. "You don't take direction very well, do you?"

Hernando joined him at the front door. Marcella hugged her friend. "I thought I'd never see you again," she said. She began to sob.

"I'm fine," Hernando replied. "Ben told me you had taken the children to St. Jude's. Why are you still here?"

Marcella pointed to the van. The front left tire was flat. A jack and tire iron lay on the ground. "I tried to fix it, but I couldn't. Without another vehicle I had no means of getting them out of here. I turned off the lights, and we hid in the basement. It was all I could think to do."

Hernando smiled. "You did the right thing," he said.

Slowly, the curious children began to emerge from the doorway at the top of the stairs. Teresa saw Egan and ran to him as fast as she could. Ben kneeled down. He scooped up the little girl in his arms. "Hey, peanut," he said. "How are you feeling?"

Teresa was all smiles. "Better."

"No more wheezing?"

She shook her head. "Nope," she said. "Watch this!" The child took a deep breath, held it for a few seconds, then blew out the air. "I can hold my breath longer than anyone else," she said proudly.

Marcella smiled. To Egan she said, "All she's been doing since you left is challenging the other children to breath holding competitions."

"Does she win?" Egan asked.

"Every time."

"That's my girl," Egan said. He cupped his hand over the child's ear and whispered. "Do me a favor?"

Teresa returned the gesture. "What?" she whispered.

"Go tell the others I said you're in charge. Make sure they're not scared. Think you can you do that for me?"

"Okay," Teresa replied. She wrapped her arms around his neck, kissed him on the cheek, then scrambled down out of his arms and ran back inside the building.

When the child was out of earshot Egan turned to Marcella. "We ran into some trouble at Le Carvery," he said. "Two of Mendoza's men are dead."

"My God," Marcella said. "What happened?"

"They tried to kill me," Hernando explained. "I protected myself. It was self defense."

Marcella shivered from fear, rubbed her arms. "This is crazy," she said. "We need to get help."

"From whom?" Hernando asked.

"The police."

"We can't do that," Egan said.

"Why not?"

"Because men like Mendoza have connections at the highest levels of law enforcement," Egan replied. "If it came down to his word against Hernando, you can guess who they would believe."

"Then what do we do?" Marcella asked.

"The plan hasn't changed," Egan said. "We need to get you and the children out of here as fast as possible."

"How?"

Egan looked toward the front gate. "We passed a daycare centre on the way here about a mile down the road. Can you get the kids there safely?"

"I think so," Marcella replied.

"Do it," Egan said. He turned to Hernando. "You should go with them."

The old man shook his head. "I'm staying here," he replied. "I've given my life to this place. If Mendoza's going to try to take it from me it's not going to be without a fight."

"You're no match for him, Hernando," Marcella said. "After what you did to his men, he'll kill you the first chance he gets."

"Then so be it," Hernando replied adamantly. "I'm not leaving."

Marcella turned to Egan. Tears welled in her eyes. "Please, Ben. Talk some sense into him. The children need him. *I* need him."

Hernando took the woman's face in his hands. "I'll be fine, Marcella. I promise."

Marcella spoke as he wiped away her tears. "You're too stubborn for your own good. You know that?"

Hernando smiled. "We both know it's never been one of my better traits."

To Ben she said, "Watch out for him. Keep him safe."

"I'll do my best," Egan replied.

Marcella shook her head. "I need more than that," she said. "I need your word."

"These men are unpredictable, Marcella," Egan

answered. "Very dangerous."

Marcella stared at Egan. "I know," she said. "But something tells me you are too."

Egan put his hand on her shoulder. "I'll do everything I can to protect Hernando," he said. "Now take the children and go. We're wasting time."

Marcella nodded. She entered the building and called out to the children. "Come on, kids," she said. "We're going on a little field trip." Inside, the children yelled and clapped with glee.

Hernando and Egan walked across the compound. "What happens now?" Hernando asked.

Egan stared at the main gate. "We wait," he said.

CHAPTER 22

DIEGO MENDOZA STEPPED into the walk-in freezer and looked down at the blood-covered bodies of his two dead enforcers. "The old man did this?" he asked.

Matias stood beside him. "Looks that way," he said.

"Where is he now?"

"We don't know."

"You're telling me he got away?"

Matias pointed to the open side door. "Through there. Salamanca and Garcia searched the factory and the grounds," he said. "They couldn't find him anywhere. He's gone."

Salamanca addressed his boss. "His car is still here. It's parked out back."

"There was another man, sir," Garcia offered.

Mendoza looked up. "Who?"

"The guy from the orphanage. The same one you had words with at the gate."

"He was here?" Mendoza asked.

"Yes, sir," Garcia said. "Salamanca and I chased after him when he ran out the employee entrance door, but…"

"But what?"

"We couldn't open the door," Garcia replied. "It was sealed shut."

"What are you talking about?" Mendoza asked.

"He did something to the door," Salamanca said. "We checked it from the outside. It's stuck to the frame."

"It's more than just stuck," Garcia corrected. "It was melted."

"What do you mean, melted?" Mendoza asked.

"Exactly that, sir," Salamanca confirmed. "Like he took a blowtorch to it, welded it shut. But that would have been impossible since we were right behind him. We tried the door. It wouldn't budge."

Mendoza turned to Matias. "Did you check it out?"

Matias nodded. "It's exactly as they say. I've never seen anything like it."

"I don't care what he did to the damn door!" Mendoza yelled. "What matters is that he and Diaz got away. That never should have happened!"

"We know where to find him, Diego," Matias said. "The old man would never leave the orphanage unprotected. He'll be there."

"Agreed," Mendoza said. "Clean up this mess, then rally the men. We're leaving now. I want that sonofabitch dead by the end of the day. And his friend too."

"Yes, sir," Matias said.

CHAPTER 23

THIRTY MINUTES INTO the drive along the alternate route the driver called out to Hallier. "Sir, we've reached the transfer point."

"Copy that," Hallier replied.

"Transfer point?" Jordan asked.

"We're switching vehicles," Hallier replied. "It's standard operating procedure." He addressed the team. "Grab your gear."

The truck braked to a stop. Voices could be heard outside; commands being issued in Spanish. The rear doors to the panel truck swung open. The DARPA commandos exited the vehicle. Beside the truck, the side door of a dark gray van slid open. The driver stepped out, saluted. "Welcome to Costa Rica, Colonel," he said.

"Collins," Hallier said, acknowledging the man as the team loaded their equipment into the transfer van. "Status report."

The in-country operative updated his superior. "I have a six-man team en route to La Fortuna per your request, sir," Collins replied. "They should be there momentarily. You want them to take up positions outside the orphanage?"

"Negative," Hallier said. "We can't risk Commander Egan knowing we're here. Tell them to wait. We'll rally up and move in tonight."

Collins nodded. "Copy that, sir. Ready to roll when you are."

Hallier turned to Jordan. "A moment, Agent Quest."

"Yes, Colonel," Jordan replied.

The two stepped away from the team and spoke privately. "How strong is your psychic connection to Commander Egan?" Hallier asked.

"Sir?" Jordan said.

Hallier looked concerned. "Unlike your ability, his is not a natural gift. We've weaponized his mind. That was by design. To be clear, we still don't know the full extent of his capabilities. We're in uncharted waters here. I need to know you can handle yourself. Your life, and most likely that of your partner, will depend on it."

"With all due respect, Colonel," Jordan replied, "I wouldn't be standing here if I couldn't."

"Good enough," Hallier said. "Because I'll need your help to take Egan down."

"What do you need me to do?"

"Create a diversion."

"How?"

"Do you think you could get inside his head? Keep him mentally occupied?"

"Probably," Jordan replied. "Why?"

"From what we observed during the crisis at the University," Hallier explained, "the commander's ability to focus his augmented defensive energy is limited. He can only use his powers to hold us at bay if his concentration is one hundred percent focused. If you can interfere with him psychically when we make our move that should give us the second or two advantage we'll need to deploy countermeasures."

"Then what? You kill him?"

"If it comes to that, yes. Remember Agent Quest, this is a matter of national security. We'll do whatever we have to do to end this. If it makes you feel any better, I'm sincerely hoping Commander Egan will surrender peacefully. He is first and foremost a decorated soldier."

"Who's being hunted by the very people who created him and trained him to kill."

Hallier was taken aback. "You're not defending his actions at the University, are you?"

Jordan shook her head. "I'm just pointing out the obvious."

"Which is?"

"You went too far."

"What is that supposed to mean?"

"That perhaps some things are best left alone. Maybe we don't need super-soldiers like Commander Egan after all."

"Spoken like a true civilian, Agent Quest," Hallier replied. "I can assure you that if you knew what I know you wouldn't feel that way. Do you have any idea how many foreign operatives are at work in this country as we speak, trying to undermine our way of life? Tens of thousands. I won't tell you the actual number because you probably wouldn't believe it. The only way we'll ever win the war against this type of subversive intelligence is to stay one step ahead of our enemies. Developing and deploying assets like Commander Egan enables us to do just that."

"The problem is he's no longer under your control, is he?" Jordan countered. "Which is exactly why we find ourselves here, right now."

Hallier folded his arms. "Let me ask you a question, agent. Do your children sleep well at night?"

Jordan nodded. "Like babies."

"Do you know why that is?"

"I'm sure you're going to tell me," Jordan replied.

"It's because people like me make sure they have nothing to worry about. They'll get up in the morning, have breakfast, go off to school... all without a care in the world. If you knew how many times we've come within a breath of losing that peace you'd probably shit yourself. You wouldn't let your children out of your sight ever again, not even for a minute. Creating soldiers like Commander Egan isn't just an ego stroke for DARPA, it's become mandatory; a necessary evil if we're to maintain our position as a world power."

Collins called out to Hallier. "Sir, we're good to go."

Hallier acknowledged the operative with a wave of his hand, then returned his attention to Jordan. "Make a call, Agent Quest. Talk to your kids. Let their voices be a reminder to you why this mission is as important as it is."

The colonel walked to the van, turned, looked back. "I'll give you one minute," he said. He opened the door and seated himself in the vehicle.

Jordan made the call.

Despite repeated attempts to reach Marissa her calls

went to voicemail.

An uneasy feeling came over her.

Something was wrong.

CHAPTER 24

MARISSA HEARD THE SIREN, saw the flashing lights of the police car in her rear-view mirror, and pulled the car over to the side of the road. In the center console her cellphone rang for the third time. The display read JORDAN. Answering the call would have to wait. Dealing with the police was the immediate priority. She would call her back in a few minutes.

"What's wrong, Marissa?" Emma asked.

"I have no idea, sweetie," Marissa replied.

The police car slowed to a stop. The officer remained in his car, watching her.

"I'll bet you were speeding," Aiden said.

"No, Aiden. I wasn't speeding," Marissa replied.

"Busted!" the boy teased.

"That's enough," Marissa said. "You two both have your seatbelts on back there?"

"Yes," the children replied in unison.

"Good. Keep them on. I don't want the officer to think you weren't wearing them."

The black SUV that had followed them from the school was nowhere in sight. Strange, Marissa thought. Over the years she had become so accustomed to the security detail following her everywhere she went with the children that she now found it unusual not to be tailed by the two-man team.

In her side mirror, Marissa watched the policeman exit his vehicle. He was dressed in plainclothes. An undercover officer, perhaps? A detective? He approached the car slowly, stopped at the back of the vehicle to inspect the taillight, then walked to her door and motioned for her to lower her window.

Marissa complied. "Good afternoon, officer," she said.

The officer smiled. "Afternoon ma'am."

Once more Marissa glanced in her side mirror. Still no sign of the security detail. She was beginning to worry. The officer's mannerism and tone weren't sitting right with her. Something about the situation felt off.

"License and registration, please," the officer asked.

"Certainly," Marissa said. She opened her purse, removed the two pieces of identification and handed them to the officer. "Why am I being stopped?" she asked. "To my knowledge I wasn't speeding."

"No ma'am," the officer replied. "That's not the issue at all." He offered no further explanation.

The cryptic conversation was starting to annoy her. "I'm going to need a reason," Marissa said.

"You have a light out."

"Excuse me?"

The officer was spending an unusually long period of time examining her identification. "One of your back lights is out."

She had taken the car in for its regularly scheduled maintenance two days ago. It was certainly possible the light bulb could have blown out in that short span of time, but the odds against that were high. "Which light is it?" Marissa asked.

"What do you mean?"

"Is it my left, center or right brake light? Turn signal indicator? I'd like to know which one is out."

The officer hesitated. "Brake light, right side," he replied.

Marissa shifted in her seat, slid her foot over the brake pedal, then glanced at the children in the rear-view mirror. "You guys okay back there?" she asked.

"Fine," Emma answered. She was glued to her phone, as usual. She looked up. "Can we go soon?"

"In a minute, honey."

"We're all going to jail," Aiden stated emphatically.

"No one's going to jail, Aiden," Marissa answered. She tapped the brake pedal lightly and looked in the rear-view mirror. The brake lights beamed bright red against the windshield of the police car. There was nothing wrong with any of lights. All were functioning normally.

"Where are you headed?" the officer asked.

Marissa stared at the policeman. "Why do you ask?" she said.

The officer's friendly tone began to change. "I suggest you answer my question," he said.

"And I suggest you show me your badge," Marissa replied.

The officer pointed to the Crown Victoria, its service lights flashing red and blue behind its front grill, dancing left to right with strobe-like effect. "Is there something about a police car you can't quite comprehend? Lights and siren not good enough for you?"

"Why did you refer to it as a police car?" Marissa asked.

"Excuse me?"

"I've never known an LAPD officer to refer to his vehicle by any term other than 'unit.'"

"That's it," the officer said. "Step out of the car now."

"I'm not leaving my vehicle until I've verified your credentials." Marissa said. She held out her hand. "This is the second time I've asked. I won't ask a third. Show me your badge."

"You're quite a piece of work, aren't you?"

"That's it," Marissa replied. She picked up her cellphone.

"Just what do you think you're doing?" the officer asked.

"Calling 911," Marissa replied. "If you're not prepared to present your identification..."

Before she could place the call, Elton Mannafort grabbed her outstretched hand, pulled her against the doorframe, removed the stun gun from the small of his back, jammed the device against her chest and pressed the trigger. In an instant, 40,000 volts of electricity shot through Marissa's body. She shook momentarily then slumped in her seat, unconscious.

Elton turned to the children. Emma and Aiden stared at him, too terrified even to speak.

"Get out," Elton said. "You're coming with me."

The children did as they were told.

Elton issued a warning. "If you scream, I'll kill you. If you try to run, I'll kill you. But before I do that, I'll kill her." He pointed to Marissa. "Nod if we understand each other."

The children complied.

"Good," Elton said. He pointed to the police car. "Get in the back seat." He nudged the boy, pushed him forward.

Aiden took Emma by the hand. "We're going," he said. "Just don't hurt my sister."

Elton shoved the stun stick into his back. "Shut up and move!" he said.

CHAPTER 25

EGAN AND HERNANDO stood at the main gate of the orphanage and watched as Marcella and the children walked single file along the side of the road in the direction of the daycare centre. "At least they'll be safe there," Hernando said. "Mendoza won't suspect we've moved them."

"They'll be coming soon," Egan said. He turned to his friend. "You should leave. I can handle Mendoza and his men by myself."

Hernando shook his head. "I'm staying. After what I did to Mendoza's men, he'll want me dead. I'm a danger to the children if I'm anywhere near them."

Egan looked around. Other than the main building, the grounds of the orphanage offered little protection against the inevitable attack they soon would be facing. "We need to fortify this place," he said. "You said you have no weapons whatsoever on the premises?"

Hernando shook his head. "None."

"All right," Egan said. "Then we'll have to improvise." He pointed to a pile of pressurized lumber stacked behind the rear of the main building. "We need to move that to the front gate, block their vehicles from entering."

"That wood was delivered by truck," Hernando said.

ompany off-loaded it using a forklift.
trips. There's no possible way we can

hing about moving it by hand?" Egan

"I don't understand."

"Remember how I helped little Teresa?" Egan said.

"Yes," Hernando said. "You healed her with your hands."

"That was nothing."

"What do you mean?"

Egan smiled. "You're going to see something now that you won't believe, Hernando. But before I do this, you need to promise me one thing."

"What's that?"

"Don't have a heart attack."

"Why would I have a—"

Egan turned and faced the enormous stack of lumber and raised his hands. His palms began to glow, rose-red.

Hernando watched in disbelief as the pile of wood began to vibrate, then lift off the ground. The old man crossed himself. "Santa Maria!" he said. "This isn't possible!"

Egan directed the pile of wood across the grounds and set it down in front of the main gate. He lowered his arms. The strange glow dissipated. Within seconds his palms had returned to normal. He looked at Hernando. "You okay?"

Hernando looked at him, slack jawed. "How did you—"

"It's a long story," Egan replied. "Let's just say I've had an upgrade or two. Remember, you promised me you wouldn't freak out."

"I promised I wouldn't have a heart attack," Hernando replied. "I said nothing about not freaking out!" Hernando was still trying to recover from the incredible telekinetic display he had just witnessed. "That pile of wood must weigh a thousand pounds," he said. "You moved it with your mind... like it was nothing."

Egan smiled. "Cool, huh?"

"How can you be so blasé?" Hernando said. "That was miraculous. What else can you do?"

"To tell you the truth, I don't think I have any limitations," Egan replied.

"Can you fly?" Hernando asked.

Egan raised a finger as if pointing out a fact. "You've got me there. Nope, can't fly. I guess that makes it Superman 1, me 0."

"What do you plan to do with the wood?"

"I'll figure that out when the time comes. Right now, we have other preparations to make."

"Such as?"

"We need to move the van into the center of the compound," Egan replied.

"I'll get the keys," Hernando said.

"How is the facility heated?"

Hernando pointed to two large white tanks at the back of the property. "Propane," he replied.

"Are they full?"

"Should be. They were topped up last week."

"Good," Egan said. "We can work with that."

"Anything else?"

"The supply shed back there. What's in it?"

"Tools."

"Can you be a smidge more specific?"

Hernando shrugged. "The usual, I guess. Handsaws, hammers, a drill, screwdrivers. Whatever I need to take care of odd jobs around the place."

"Collect it all. Bring it into the main building."

"You've got it."

Egan looked up at the bruised-purple sky. "We're losing daylight," he said. "My guess is they'll make their move when darkness falls."

"That's what I would do," Hernando agreed.

Egan put his hand on his friend's shoulder. "There's still time for you to leave. Go down the road to the daycare. Join Marcella and the children."

Hernando shook his head. "Not gonna happen," he replied.

"You sure you're ready for this?" Egan asked.

"I've never been more ready for anything in my whole life," the old man replied.

CHAPTER 26

DIEGO MENDOZA RETURNED to his office, opened his desk drawer, removed the Glock 22, checked the clip, chambered a round and slipped the weapon into his waistband.

He turned to Matias. "I didn't think the old man had it in him," he said, referring to the two dead enforcers Hernando Diaz had killed and whose bodies lay in the freezer. "That took balls."

Matias nodded. "Perhaps he's better equipped to handle himself than we've given him credit for."

"That not what concerns me."

"Oh?"

"The guy at the orphanage," Diego said. "Have you seen him before?"

Matias shook his head. "Never. Why?"

"Don't you find it rather unusual that he suddenly shows up out of nowhere?"

"You thinking he's a pro? Protection for hire, maybe?"

"Possible, but unlikely," Diego replied. "Diaz wouldn't know the first thing about finding a pro, much less hiring one."

"It wouldn't be hard. The country's full of them. But he'd need to know who to ask."

"And that would be?"

Matias thought for a moment. "Tomas Consuelos."

Consuelos was head of the Cabeza de Muerte, a high-level street gang. The crew had come to Mendoza's attention recently when the news that Mara Salvatrucha, more commonly known as MS-13, had expanded their operation from El Salvador into Costa Rica and begun recruiting poor Costa Rican teens into their fold. Word had also come down that MS-13 had set its sights on taking over Diego's cocaine empire, and that Tomas Consuelos had already set a plan in motion to make that happen.

"I should have put a bullet in that bastard's head years ago," Diego said.

"It's not too late," Matias said. "Perhaps we should pay him a visit. Find out what he knows."

"He's too well protected," Diego replied. "We'd never get near him."

"What if he thought you were willing to make a deal?"

"Meaning?"

"Tell him you know what he has planned and that you're willing to discuss forming an alliance."

"He's not stupid. He'll figure he's being set up. When he does, we'll be at war."

"We'll be at war soon enough," Matias said. "Right now, what you need to know is whether Diaz's man is part of his crew."

"An American working for Consuelos?" Diego said. "Not likely."

"You have a better theory?"

"No," Diego said. He paused, considered the suggestion. "If we're going to do this it needs to be one-to-one. And the invitation needs to come from me personally."

Matias agreed. "Do you know how to reach him?"

"No," Diego said, "but I know who does."

He picked up his desk phone, placed a call.

"Hello?"

"Pérez, it's Diego Mendoza."

Alonzo Pérez's company, Sun Tropic, was the largest distributor of fresh fruit in Costa Rica. He also provided the ground transportation for Diego's cocaine supply across the country in his specially outfitted trucks.

"Diego," Alonzo said. "To what do I owe the pleasure?"

"I need you to set up a meeting."

"With?"

"Tomas Consuelos."

Pérez paused. "Do you have a death wish, my friend?" he asked.

"I'm just looking for information."

"Concerning?"

"An urgent matter."

Pérez laughed. "You're being evasive, Diego."

"No, just careful."

"If that's the case, are you open to taking advice from an old friend?"

"Depends on the advice."

"Stay as far away from Tomas as you can," Pérez

warned. "Nothing good could come from a meeting with him where you are concerned."

"I've heard the rumors."

"They're not rumors, Diego. He is making plans."

"Meaning?"

"Let's just say you'd be wise to have someone watching your back twenty-four seven."

"That puts me a difficult position," Diego said.

"How so?"

"I have a problem that needs to be dealt with."

Alonzo paused. "How many men do you need?"

"Four should be enough. But not amateurs. I need professionals."

"I can arrange that. Who's the target?"

"You wouldn't know him."

"Try me."

"Hernando Diaz."

"The old man who runs the orphanage?"

"Yes."

"He's one of my customers. He's harmless. How could he possibly be a problem for you?"

"He's not," Diego replied. "But there's someone staying with him who is. I think this guy's been hired for personal protection. I need him taken out quickly and quietly. Diaz has something I want. I'm getting tired of waiting."

"Very well," Alonzo said. "Your reasons are your reasons. That's good enough for me. Where and when should we meet?"

"You're coming too?"

"Yes," Pérez said. "You've aroused my curiosity."

"All right. The orphanage. Seven P.M."

"We'll be there."

"And Alonzo?"

"Yes?"

"Warn your people. Make sure they know this man is not be taken for granted."

"What makes you say that, Diego?"

"Instinct."

CHAPTER 27

THE EXPRESSION ON HALLIER'S face told Chris the colonel was very upset. He watched the soldier walk back to the truck, climb aboard, and slam the door.

He walked up to Jordan and glanced back at the truck. "I see that conversation went well. What did you say to piss him off?"

"We had a difference of opinion."

"Over what?"

"Commander Egan."

"What's the issue?"

"Nothing important. Philosophical differences, I guess."

"You having second thoughts about the mission?"

"No," Jordan said. "The commander has to be stopped. There's no way around that."

"What does he want you do?"

"Get inside his head, create a diversion."

"That shouldn't be a problem for you."

"It won't."

"Then what's the concern?"

"He plans to kill him. I'm not sure that's necessary."

"It's not your call, Jordan. It's Hallier's."

"I know."

"This is a DARPA operation, not FBI," Chris stressed. "We're playing in their sandbox, not ours. It's

148

their game, so it's their rules." He studied Jordan's face. "Something else is bugging you. What is it?"

"I don't know."

"Yeah, you do. Fess up."

"I tried to call home to talk to the kids."

"And?"

"I can't reach Marissa."

Chris shrugged. "Maybe she's just away from the phone and can't pick up. No big deal."

"Something's not right."

"The woman is in charge of two kids when you're not home. She might just have her hands full."

"That's not it."

"Then what is?"

"I code-called her."

"You what?"

"We have a system," Jordan explained. "If I can't reach her on the first call and need to talk to her urgently, I'll call her back two more times, one call right after the other. Three missed calls from me means drop whatever you're doing and get back to me immediately."

"And you tried her three times?"

Jordan nodded. "No reply."

Chris took out his phone, handed it to Jordan. "Punch in her number."

Jordan entered Marissa's cell number. Chris placed the call. The phone rang and rang.

"Voicemail," he said.

"I'm telling you… something's not right."

"I wouldn't get too worked up about it, J. She could

have any number of reasons for not picking up. Try her again in an hour."

Hallier rolled down his window, called out. "Let's go."

Jordan and Chris walked back to the truck. "I'm sure Marissa and the kids are just fine," Chris said as they climbed aboard. "But if you're that concerned use your abilities. Connect with her."

"I don't have much of a choice," Jordan said. "It's bothering me too much. I can't concentrate."

"Then do it."

Jordan closed her eyes, focused, and reached out to Marissa. In the darkness of her mind, it was the emotional connection that struck her first and hardest. She saw the image of her housekeeper. Her eyes were closed. Her body lay at an odd angle, yet she was not asleep. Her vital force was low. The energy emanating from within her suggested she was in a trance-like state. It was then that the movie began to play, flashes of memory communicated from her subconscious mind: The car stopping… the man at the window… the missed calls… then the incredible jolt of electricity which shook her body and rendered her unconscious, delivering her into the dreamlike state which Jordan had now entered.

Jordan broke the connection. "Oh, God," she said.

"What's wrong?" Chris asked.

"It's Marissa."

"Is she hurt?"

"She's been attacked."

"What about the kids? Are they all right?"

Jordan started to panic. "I don't see them. Oh, God! Emma and Aiden... my babies!"

"Calm down, Jordan," Chris urged.

"If Marissa's not watching over them..."

"I've got this," Chris said. He took out his cellphone, placed a call.

"Federal Bureau of Investigation."

"This is Special Agent Chris Hanover. I need an emergency location trace on the following cell number: (310) 555-2311. The phone is registered to Marissa DeSola."

"One moment." The response came seconds later. "The number is active and in Brentwood, California. The signal appears to be stationary."

"Dispatch agents and LAPD to the location immediately," Chris ordered. "Person in distress."

"Copy that, agent. Contacting them now."

Chris hung up the phone. He turned to Jordan. "They're on their way. Everything's going to be all right."

Jordan said nothing. She stared out the side window of the van.

The reality of the situation struck her.

She was thousands of miles away.

Back home, an unknown danger was threatening her family.

And there was not a damn thing she could do about it.

CHAPTER 28

AGNES WATTS MADE IT her business to know everything that was going on in the neighborhood. The Reese's, the young couple who lived behind her, he a sales executive, she a nurse, loved the new hot tub they had purchased three weeks ago. They spend at least an hour in it every night, usually between the hours of 8:00 and 9:00 P.M., sometimes together, often with other couples. The hot tub Agnes didn't mind. It was the lack of swimwear that irritated her. She knew this because she had a clear view of the couple's backyard from her bedroom window.

Vera Lang, the widow who lived across street, had started seeing someone new. The fledgling relationship had been burning bright for three weeks now. When Kelly Mathews, Agnes's next door neighbor, raised the subject while they shopped for groceries together at the local Food Emporium, Agnes was quick to point out that Vera had been receiving a visit from her new flame at least once a week for the last year prior to her husband's passing. She shared this important update while examining the contents of Kelly's shopping cart, noting the lack of fresh fruit and vegetables and the abundance of processed foods and sugary snacks. Carbohydrate Kelly, as Agnes called her behind her back, hung on every word as Agnes brought her up to speed on the latest gossip, preceding every statement by saying 'not that it's any of my business.'

Barney and his sister Kiki, Agnes' much-loved Chihuahua's, really had to poop. The dogs barked non-stop and ran back and forth from the kitchen to the front door, communicating the urgent message to Agnes that if she didn't rectify the situation within the next minute or less that any responsibility for the ensuing mess they would make in the house would be on her, not them.

"All right, we're going," Agnes said. She leashed the dogs and unlocked the front door. Kiki, always having been the alpha of the two siblings, squeezed past her brother and made a beeline for the front yard. Barney strolled out the front door, sniffed out a preferred spot, and did his business.

After the dogs had happily relieved themselves, they began pawing at Agnes's pant leg, informing their mom that they were ready to go for their regularly scheduled afternoon walk. Kiki strained on her leash, while Barney walked calmly at Agnes' side. Then Barney did something completely out of character. He stopped, looked down the empty street, growled and began to bark madly. Despite Agnes' attempts to calm the dog he would not settle down. His attention seemed to be drawn to a black SUV parked on the street several houses down the road. Agnes knew the make and model of most of the cars that visited her street. She had never seen this vehicle before.

Mitchell Dawson, who was walking his Great Dane, Prince, waved at Agnes from across the street. The two often walked their dogs together which gave Mitchell the opportunity to catch up on the latest neighborhood happenings, compliments of Agnes. When Agnes didn't acknowledge him he became concerned. It was not like her to snub anyone, much less pass up the chance to gossip to anybody who would listen. Mitchell and Prince crossed the street.

"How are you, Agnes?" Mitchell asked. Prince lowered his massive head and sniffed Kiki's backside.

"Fine, I guess," Agnes replied.

Mitchell laughed. "That didn't sound very convincing. Is everything all right?"

Agnes drew his attention to the black SUV. "Have you ever seen that car around here before?" she asked.

Mitchell shrugged. "Can't say as I have. Whoever owns it is probably just visiting. Why?"

"I don't know," Agnes said. "But it's got Barney really worked up."

"Barney has cataracts."

"So?"

"Maybe the old boy is seeing things that aren't there," Mitchell said. "Remember our poodle, Molly? Died three years ago. Poor girl couldn't see two feet in front of her face after her eyesight started to go. Barked at everything she couldn't make out."

Agnes disagreed. "Barney's vision isn't that bad yet."

Mitchell folded his arms. "If you say so." He stared at the SUV. Barney continued to bark.

"I know that tone," Agnes said. "He's upset.

Something's got him spooked."

"You're reading too much into it," Mitchell replied. "I wouldn't worry about it."

"Maybe we should have a closer look."

"It's just a car, Agnes."

As Agnes walked down the street, Barney pulled harder on his leash. Kiki trotted beside her big brother.

Mitchell and Prince followed reluctantly, staying a few paces behind the trio.

As they approached the vehicle, Jim Stafford, a neighbor, walked out of his house and down his front steps. The SUV was parked in front of his home. The car had also gotten his attention.

Agnes and Mitchell stopped. "Everything okay, Jim?" Mitchell asked.

Stafford walked over, petted the dogs. "I don't know," he said. He looked in the car's direction, scratched his head. "I'm not sure what to make of this."

"What do you mean?" Agnes asked.

"A cop stopped it over an hour ago," Stafford said. "An unmarked squad car. I was looking out the window when I saw him light it up and pull it over. A plainclothes officer got out, talked to the driver for a minute, maybe less, then left. Thing is, the car hasn't moved an inch since then."

"That's odd," Mitchell said.

"I'm going to check it out," Jim said. He walked to the passenger side of the SUV, tried to look in, couldn't. "Windows are too heavily tinted," he reported. "I can't see inside." He tapped on the glass. "Hey," he said.

"Anybody in there?"

No response.

"You think the cop arrested whoever was in the car?" Mitchell asked.

"Could be," Jim said. "I wasn't watching for very long. But if that was the case, wouldn't you think they'd have sent a flatbed to pick it up? They'd take it to the impound, right? They wouldn't just leave it sitting here."

"That would make sense," Agnes said.

Stafford walked around to the driver's side, wrapped on the window.

Nothing.

Barney growled.

"This doesn't make any sense," Jim said. "Who would leave an expensive car like this abandoned at the side of the road?"

"Check the door," Mitchell suggested. "See if it's locked."

Stafford hesitated. "I'm not sure if I should do that."

"Why not?" Agnes asked. "If it's unlocked, you can check the glove box for a vehicle registration." By now her curiosity to know who the car belonged to was killing her.

Stafford knocked on the window again, harder this time.

Still no response.

"I guess it couldn't hurt to look inside," he agreed. He pulled up the handle, opened the door, then jumped back in horror. "Jesus!" he yelled.

"What is it, Jim?" Mitchell asked. "What's wrong?"

Jim Stafford backed away from the SUV. He stood in the middle of the street, visibly shaken, and pointed inside the car. "They're dead," he said. "They're both dead!"

CHAPTER 29

MARISSA DeSOLA AWOKE in the car, disoriented and confused. The sudden shock to her system from the high pulse frequency of the stun gun had depleted her of all energy. She groaned, lolled her head to the left, then right. She tried to grip the steering wheel, use it to pull herself up in the seat, but lost her balance and fell back. The electrical charge delivered by the weapon had depleted her blood sugar stores and converted them to lactic acid, making voluntary movement nearly impossible. She raised her hand clumsily, opened her blouse, looked down and saw the two small burn marks left on her skin by the electrical discharge from the weapons electrodes. Her attacker had thrust the device against her chest, pulled the trigger, immobilized her.

When finally she pulled herself out of the brain fog and regain control of her body, Marissa turned in her seat to check on the children.

Aiden and Emma were gone.

Seized by adrenaline, Marissa unbuckled her seat belt, threw open the door, jumped out and ran around the car, searching frantically for any sign of the children.

Nothing.

The rear passenger door was open. Emma's cellphone lay on the floor. The children's backpacks lay propped up on the seat.

"Oh, God! Oh, God!" Marissa cried. In her rising panic she ran up and down the street, calling out their names. "Emma! Aiden!"

Marissa was out of her mind with worry. She fell to her knees and began to cry.

Mindy Aberfoyle had been sitting in her favorite reading chair, engrossed in the story, when she heard the commotion outside. She looked out her living room window and saw the distraught woman kneeling in the street. The retired nurse quickly pulled a throw blanket off her couch, grabbed her cellphone from the side table, slipped on shoes and rushed out the door.

Marissa was inconsolable. Mindy threw the blanket around her, kneeled beside her. "Honey, what's wrong?" she asked.

"Taken," Marissa replied.

"What do you mean, honey? Who was taken?"

Marissa began to rock back and forth. Whatever had happened to the woman, it had been a horrifying emotional experience. Mindy could see she was going into shock. She had to pull her back from the brink as quickly as possible.

"What's your name, sweetie?" Mindy asked.

"M-Marissa."

Mindy began to rub Marissa's hands and arms. The tactile sensation kept her engaged. "Marissa, my name is Mindy. I'm a nurse. I'm going to help you. But you've got to stay will me, okay? Can you do that for me?"

Marissa looked up, nodded.

"Good girl," Mindy said. "You said someone was

taken. Who was it?" While Mindy waited for Marissa to respond she powered up her cellphone, dialed emergency services.

"911," the dispatcher answered. "Do you require police, fire or ambulance?"

"Police and ambulance," Misty replied.

"What is your location?"

"1108 Bayly Street, Brentwood."

"The children," Marissa said.

"Someone took your children?" Mindy asked. She stared at the car, saw its driver and rear passenger doors were wide open. She put the pieces together. "Were they kidnapped?"

"I think so... yes."

"How many children, Marissa?"

"Two."

"I need their names," Mindy said.

"Emma and Aiden Quest."

Mindy heard clicking sounds in the background of the call. The dispatcher was typing on her keyboard. "Are you getting this?" Mindy asked.

"I am," the operator replied. "Tender age male and female. Suspected abduction. Your call has been escalated. Police should be at your location within minutes."

"Minutes?" Mindy yelled. "Two children have been kidnapped! We don't have minutes. We have seconds!"

"I understand," the dispatcher said. "Police are on their way. Stay on the line with me until they arrive."

"You need to issue an Amber Alert!"

"We will."

Marissa stared vacantly at Mindy. Her voice cracked when she spoke. "I was responsible for them," she said.

Mindy held Marissa's wrist, took her pulse, racing. She checked her eyes. Her pupils were wide, dilated. The woman was terrified. "You need to calm down, honey," she urged.

Sirens in the distance. Help was on the way.

Marissa gripped Mindy's hand, held it tight. "Police," she whispered.

"Yes, honey," Mindy assured her. "The police are coming."

A black and white LAPD squad car raced around the corner at the foot of the street, lights flashing, siren blaring, followed closely by an unmarked car.

Marissa shook her head. "No… Police took the children."

Mindy couldn't believe what she had just heard. "What did you say?"

Marissa's grip began to weaken. Mindy knew the signs. She was losing her.

"It… was… the police," Marissa said. Her hand fell to the ground.

Mindy tapped her hand against Marissa's face, tried to revive her. "Marissa… Marissa… wake up!"

The police cars arrived on the scene, screeched to a halt just feet away from the two women. The uniformed officers exited their vehicle and ran to their aid. The doors to the unmarked sedan opened. The men stepped out, identified themselves. "FBI," they told the police officers. "I'm Special Agent Laird. This is Special Agent Cummins. We'll take it from here."

An ambulance rounded the corner, sped to the scene, blocked the road.

Mindy held the stranger in her arms. Marissa had told her the police had taken the children. Impossible, she thought. That simply couldn't be. What the hell was going on?

Mindy provided Agent Laird with what little information Marissa had shared with her before she succumbed to shock and fainted. "That's all I know," she said. "Two children, taken by the police."

"We need more than that," Laird said. Cummins had been conferring with LAPD while his partner interviewed the nurse. "There've been no calls to this street," he reported. "No record of a traffic stop."

"Why would she lie?" Mindy asked. "That makes no sense."

The ambulance attendant lifted Marissa onto the gurney, checked her vitals. "She's thready," he said. "We need to move. Now."

"Go," Agent Laird said. "We'll take her statement at Emerg."

The paramedic nodded. "Meet you there."

The agent turned his attention back to Mindy. "Do you know the victim, ma'am?"

"No, I don't," Mindy replied. She pointed to her home. "I live right there. I heard her scream and ran outside to see if I could help." She paused.

"What is it?" Laird asked.

"I just realized something."

"What's that?"

"We've had a rash of burglaries in the area lately, parcel deliveries being stolen right off the front step."

Agent Laird looked puzzled and more than a little upset. "What has that got to do with…"

"My husband just installed a RING system. You know, one of those doorbell cameras. Maybe it recorded the whole event."

"Can you access the footage?"

"Yes. I can log into my account, view it online."

"We need to see that footage right away."

"Of course," Mindy said. "Come with me."

The agents accompanied Mindy into her home as the ambulance siren blared to life.

CHAPTER 30

HERNANDO RUMMAGED THROUGH the supplies shed, gathered as many items as he could carry in his arms at one time, then hurried back to the main building and set the items on the front steps. Several trips later, everything that could be used in their defense had been removed. Among the items he had scavenged were a toolbox, boxes of nails, gallons of wood stain intended for use on the new fence, a large steel bucket full of broken ceramic floor tiles, propane cylinders from the barbecue, two large spools of electrical wire, a jerry can of gasoline and a spare battery from the van.

Egan approved of the haul. "I can work with this," he said.

"Now what?" Hernando asked.

"Now we make their visit very uncomfortable." Egan grabbed a pair of wire cutters from the toolbox, handed them to Hernando. "Start with the wire. I'll need as many lengths as you can cut. Make them about twenty feet long and bare the wire at both ends. I'll set up the yard."

"Will do."

Egan grabbed the propane cylinders and ran to the stack of pressurized lumber he had positioned in front of the main gate. He moved several of the long posts aside, buried one of the two cylinders among the timbers and re-stacked the wood. Next, he ran to the van, pushed it away from the main building into the middle of the yard, opened the side door, and laid the second propane cylinder on the back seat.

Hernando met him at the van. In his hand he held a dozen lengths of the prepared electrical wire. "Ready," he said.

"Good." Egan said. "First, we'll need the gasoline." Hernando returned with the jerry can. Egan poured a thin line of the fuel over the tank safety valve, across the floor of the van and onto the ground. He forced one end of the bared electrical wire into the small pool of fuel at his feet. "Cover the wire with dirt and run the line inside."

"You've got it," Hernando replied.

Egan ran to the woodpile with the gas can, repeated the process, buried the second length of electrical wire with loose dirt, then ran it back to the main building.

Both propane cylinders were ready.

"Grab the wood stain. Throw in as many nails and pieces of broken tile as you can." Egan said. He pointed to two large open areas on the grounds. "We'll need one there, and one there. Leave the lids off. Same drill. One end of the wire goes in the liquid, then bury the line back to the building."

Hernando asked, "You've done this before?"

Egan smiled. "You could say that."

"When Mendoza arrives, he'll bring a small army with him."

Egan nodded. "Probably."

"You're not worried?"

"Just about you."

"I'll be okay."

"Damn right," Egan said. "Marcella and the kids are waiting for you at the daycare. You better be there for them when this is over."

"Don't worry, I will."

"There's a good chance the place is going to need a few renovations by the time we're done."

"It was ready for a new coat of paint."

"You'll probably need a new van, too."

"I was thinking more along the line of a minibus."

Egan looked around the property. "You've got a real nice place here, Hernando."

"I know," the old man said. "Seems a shame we have to blow it up."

CHAPTER 31

AIDEN HELD HIS SISTER'S HAND. "Where are you taking us?" he asked.

Elton Mannafort glanced at the children in the rear-view mirror, said nothing.

"Who are you?" Aiden asked.

Still no reply.

Emma piped up. "Our mom is an FBI agent, you know. Do you have any idea how totally screwed you are?"

"Tell them to shut up," Elton said.

"Why? They're not going to listen to me."

"Do you really want to listen to them blather on for the next hundred miles?"

"They'll settle down."

"And if they don't?"

"I'll deal with it."

"Like you dealt with the old man?"

"If it comes to that, yes."

Aiden and Emma stared at Elton, listened as he carried on the conversation with himself.

Elton spoke to the children. "I strongly recommend you sit quietly and behave yourselves. We have a long way to go."

Aiden whispered to his sister. "He's fruitier than Fruit Loops."

"Totally whackadoodle," Emma replied.

Aiden looked for a door handle to open, couldn't find one. A hard, flat plastic panel had replaced the backseat door wall. Even the passenger windows had been modified to prevent escape. Vertical steel bars obstructed his view. By design, the seat was cramped and uncomfortable. A plexiglass panel, reinforced with wire mesh, separated them from their captor. They were, for all intents and purposes, in a miniature jail.

"What did you do to Marissa?" Aiden asked.

"Nothing," Elton replied.

"Bullshit!"

Elton turned, glanced at the boy. "Does your mother permit you to use that kind of language with adults?"

"Only if he's an asshole," Aiden said. "Which you are."

"She'll be fine."

"That's not what I asked."

Elton picked up the stun stick from the passenger seat, held it up. "I gave her a little jolt with this, knocked her out. She's probably wide awake by now and none the worse for wear."

"What kind of sicko kidnaps a couple of kids?" Aiden asked. He was purposely trying to irritate the man, get under his skin.

"The same kind who won't hesitate to kill your sister if you don't shut up," Elton replied.

Aiden wanted to continue pressing the man, but something in the tone of his voice told him he was serious. He wouldn't put Emma's life in jeopardy, not for anything. He would have to wait it out. Besides, he knew it was only a matter of time before they would be found. What the jerk didn't know was that he already had two major strikes against him from the very minute he'd gotten himself into this mess. First, the Federal Bureau of Investigation didn't take too kindly to someone messing with one of their own, least of all a child. Second, he had underestimated their mother's celebrity as a renowned psychic. Once word got out about the kidnapping every news agency in the country would blanket the airwaves with the story. Their pictures would be everywhere. There wouldn't be a two-bit town or major city across the nation that wouldn't be on the lookout for them. There was, yet again, another advantage they had over the moron he didn't know about: their mother had prepared them for just such an emergency.

Years ago, the tragic death of their father and grandparents had left an indelible mark on their family. When the children were old enough to understand, Jordan sat them down and made them fully aware of the privileged station in life they had inherited by being born a Quest. She had insisted the children learn how to handle themselves. Like his mother, Aiden had proven himself to be a gifted athlete, earning his first-degree junior black belt at Rising Sun Martial Arts Academy in a record four years. It had taken his instructor five. Emma had not followed her brother into the martial arts, but her flexibility, core strength and an uncanny sense of balance had made her one of the nations top competitive gymnasts. Her coaches, wholly impressed with the young girl, had already discussed her potential to compete at the Olympic level. Plans were underway to make that dream a reality.

"You never answered my first question," Aiden repeated.

"Which was?"

"Where are you taking us?"

Elton refused to be intimidated by the boy. "You'll know when we get there," he replied.

"Why won't you tell me?" Aiden pressed. "You scared? I'll bet you are. You should be."

"The country."

"Where *specifically*?"

"My place."

They had left the city behind now, hit the Interstate. Aiden looked out the window, tried to discern familiar landmarks, saw none. He had absolutely no idea where they were.

"You'll like it," Elton said. "Its a great place for kids. Plenty of fresh air, lots of room to run around. You're going to love it."

"No, we won't."

"Sure you will. It might take a little getting used to, but you'll grow to love it."

"You know you're completely screwed, right?"

Elton began to rock back and forth in his seat. "I told you," he said. "The little shit is going to ruin it for both of us."

"Don't worry about it. Once he sees the place, he'll

be fine."

"So *you* say."

"That's right. And my opinion is the only one that counts."

"This wasn't a good idea and you know it."

"The bitch has to pay for what she did."

"You could have handled her any number of ways. Instead, you took her kids. That was stupid."

"It'll teach her a lesson she'll never forget."

"You know what you'll have to do when we get there, don't you?"

"There's plenty of time for that."

"You said the same thing about Carnie Schumacher until the cops broke the door down. Look what happened after that!"

Elton paused. "I suppose you're right."

"Of course, I'm right. I'm *always* right. We can't let that happen again."

Elton turned his attention back to Aiden. "It's going to be okay."

"What's going to be okay?" Aiden asked.

Elton checked his side mirror, executed a lane change, then set the cruise control to the posted speed limit.

"Everything," he replied.

CHAPTER 32

MINDY ABERFOYLE WELCOMED FBI Special Agents Jim Laird and Bill Cummins into her home. "My computer's in the den," she said. The agents followed her as she hurried down the hallway past the kitchen, living and dining rooms, pushed open the double French doors, sat down at her desk, flipped open the lid to her PC and entered her password. The computer screen flickered to life.

"I can access the doorbell's video footage from the app," Mindy said. She logged into the RING cloud server, found the camera labeled FRONT DOOR and launched the saved video.

Watching the video, the agents observed Marissa stop her vehicle outside Mindy's house and wait for the police car to pull in behind her. Seconds later, the unmarked sedan, its grill lights flashing, came into view and stopped a few feet behind the SUV. Two children could be seen in the back seat of the car.

"Did you see the police car pull up?" Agent Laird asked.

Mindy shook her head. "I'm seeing this for the first time too. I was drawn to the sound of a woman screaming." She pointed to the screen. "By the time I ran outside the police car was gone and Marissa was on the ground. I never saw the children until now." The nurse covered her mouth. "Oh, God," she said. "Those poor kids must be frightened to death."

"Can you download this footage?" Agent Cummins asked.

Mindy nodded. "I can save the video to my PC and send you the file."

"Thank you. We'll need it right away."

"Of course," Mindy replied.

To his partner, Laird said, "Can I speak with you privately?"

Cummins nodded.

"Ms. Aberfoyle, would you excuse us for just a moment?" Laird asked.

"Certainly," Mindy said.

The agents walked down the hall, entered the kitchen. Laird leaned against the counter, folded his arms. "What do you think?" he asked.

"I'd say we're in pretty good shape," Cummins replied. "Were it not for the doorbell cam we'd have nothing to go on."

"I didn't see him touch the car. Did you?"

Cummins shook his head.

"So much for prints."

"Regardless," Cummins said, "we'll have Evidence Response go over it. We might get lucky."

"The video capture of the UNSUB and the Quest children is very clear. Good enough to use for an Amber Alert."

Cummins nodded. "We'll get it over the air right away."

Laird agreed. "We need to get to the hospital and talk to Marissa DeSola. Maybe she can help fill in the blanks."

"Better brace yourself, Jim. There'll be a lot of eyeballs on this one, all the way to the top."

"I know. Quest is the darling of the Director."

"And for good reason," Cummins qualified. "She helped saved his daughters' lives years ago."

"I'm not taking anything away from he," Laird said. "She's a damn fine agent. Buy why the hell would anyone want to target her kids?"

"We've all made enemies along the way. It comes with the territory. I can think of more than a few bad guys who wouldn't mind taking a shot at either of us."

Mindy's sneakers squeaked on the hardwood floor as she left her office and walked down the hall. Out of respect for the agent's privacy she rapped twice on the wall before entering the kitchen. She held up a flash drive. "I made a copy of the video for you," she said. "I hope it helps."

"It's critical," Agent Laird said. "Thank you."

"Have you heard any more about Marissa? Is she okay?"

"Not yet," Cummins replied. "We're on our way to the hospital now."

"If it's not too much to ask, would you give her my regards?"

"We'll be happy to."

Hearing the front door open, Mindy stepped out of the kitchen and into the hallway. Ron, her husband, had arrived home. "How was your golf game, dear?" she asked.

"Excellent," Ron replied. He closed the door behind him. "Shot an eighty. Hey, did you know there's an unmarked cop car parked in front of our—"

He stopped short as Laird and Cummins stepped into the hallway behind his wife.

"Mindy, what's going on?" Ron asked. "Is everything all right?"

"Everything's fine, honey," Mindy replied. "These men are with the FBI."

"FBI?"

The agents produced their identification. "Your wife has been helping us with an investigation," Laird said.

"Investigation?" Ron asked. He looked puzzled. He was still trying to process what two federal agents were doing in his house.

"It's a long story," Mindy said. "Let me make you a cup of tea. I'll tell you all about it."

"Better make it a scotch," Ron replied.

Agent Cummins smiled. "It's nothing to worry about, Mr. Aberfoyle. Like your wife says, she'll fill you in on what happened." The agents walked to the vestibule, opened the front door. "We have to be on our way."

"If I can be of any further help please don't hesitate to contact me," Mindy said.

"We will," Laird replied. "Thank you again. Good day, Mr. Aberfoyle."

Ron had poured himself a drink. He raised his glass.

"Agents."

Mindy watched the man leave, then closed the door.

"Someone's had an interesting day," Ron said.

"You don't know the half of it," Mindy replied.

The FBI's Evidence Response Team had arrived, cordoned off the street and had started to process the SUV when one of the investigator's called out. "Found something under the front passenger seat," he said. He held up a pink cellphone.

"Is it password protected?" Laird asked.

The investigator tried the phone, nodded.

"Get it unlocked ASAP."

"You got it."

Every second lost between now and when the Quest children was found was critical.

Laird put the car into gear. The agents sped away.

One person, perhaps their most important witness of all, remained to be interviewed: Marissa DeSola.

No sooner had they rounded the corner than his cell phone rang. He checked the display.

Laird turned to his partner. "It's Dunn."

The Director of the FBI was calling.

CHAPTER 33

SPECIAL AGENTS LAIRD AND CUMMINS arrived at Angel of Mercy Hospital, entered the Emergency department and identified themselves to the duty nurse. "We're looking for one of your patients, Marissa DeSola," Laird said. "You would have admitted her about thirty minutes ago."

The nurse typed the name into her computer, then referred to the red, blue and yellow directional lines painted on the Emergency ward floor. "She's in recovery." She pointed down the hall. "Follow the yellow line through the double doors. Ms. DeSola is in Bed 4."

"Thank you," Laird said.

The curtains were drawn around Marissa's bed. Laird parted them slightly, saw Marissa sitting up. Her eyes were closed. "Ms. DeSola?" he asked.

Marissa turned, looked his way. Her stare was vacant. "Yes?"

Laird presented his credentials and pulled back the curtain just enough to allow the men access to her bedside. "My name is Special Agent Jim Laird. This is my partner, Special Agent Bill Cummins. We're with the FBI."

Marissa's eyes brightened. She leaned forward. "You found Aiden and Emma?"

This was the shitty part of the job, Laird thought. He glanced at his partner, then back at the woman. "Not yet, ma'am," he replied. "But we're working on it."

"I feel so stupid," Marissa said. "I thought he was a real policeman. He was driving a police car."

"Don't blame yourself, ma'am," Cummins said. "It wasn't your fault."

"My phone," Marissa said. "It's in the car. I need to speak to their mother, tell her what's happened."

"We'll take care of that for you," Laird said. "First, we need to ask you a few questions. Would that be all right?"

"Of course."

"Can you describe the man who attacked you?"

Marissa shook her head. "It all happened so fast."

"Did anything about him strike you as strange or unusual?" Cummins asked.

"How do you mean?"

"A scar on his face perhaps, a physical deformity, uncommon mannerisms?"

Marissa thought for a moment. "There was one thing."

"What's that?" Cummins asked.

"He had a small tattoo, right here." Marissa pointed to the inside of her left wrist. "I caught a glimpse of it when he grabbed my hand."

"Could you describe it?"

"A bird. A swallow, perhaps. Yes, that was it. A swallow."

"That's helpful," Laird said. "Anything else?"

"I asked him twice to show me his badge. He refused."

"He probably didn't have one."

"I must have pushed him too hard and set him off. That's when he did this." Marissa lowered the neck of her hospital gown just enough to show the agents the two small marks on her chest.

"Those are electrode burns," Cummins said. "He used a stun stick to knock you out."

"My body just gave out," Marissa said. "If only I could have fought it, I could have protected the children."

Cummins shook his head. "That would have been impossible. Once the weapon touched your body, and he pressed the trigger, it was all over. There was absolutely nothing you could do to defend yourself against the effect of the shock."

Marissa was close to tears. "Jordan trusted me to keep the children safe. I failed her *and* them."

Laird spoke. "You did no such thing, Ms. DeSola. This attack wasn't random by any means. It's clear that this man targeted you and Agent Quest's children."

"I should have known something was wrong."

"What makes you say that?" Cummins asked.

"They were no longer behind us."

"I don't follow," Laird said. "Who was no longer behind you?"

"Our security detail."

"You have personal protection?" Cummins asked.

Marissa nodded. "Sentinel Executive Protection.

Jordan's father employed them when he was alive. They've been protecting the Quest family ever since."

"And one of their operatives was assigned to you today?"

"Two of them, actually. They followed us after we left the school. They're there every day. It's called shadow protection. They don't make themselves known to us, which of course is the point, and their presence might not be obvious to anyone else. But after all these years of being followed I know them when I see them." Marissa noticed the concerned look on the agents' faces. "Why do you ask? Did something happen to them? Are they all right?"

"We don't know," Laird replied. "We weren't aware of this."

"I need to ask this," Cummins said, "so please don't be offended."

"All right," Marissa said.

"Could your security detail have had something to do with this?"

"What do you mean?"

Cummins explained. "If they were following you like they should have been, they would have seen your car being pulled over and probably intervened, yet they didn't."

Laird nodded, supported his partner. "Agent Cummins has a point."

Marissa shook her head. "I can't believe they would ever allow any harm to come to the children."

"Unfortunately, in our line of work we see good

people go bad all the time," Cummins said.

Marissa's face brightened when a familiar face suddenly joined the two men. FBI Director Andrew Dunn had arrived. The agents stepped aside as he leaned in and gave her a gentle hug.

"How are you, Marissa?" Dunn asked.

"Scared to death," Marissa replied. "He took the children."

"Aiden and Emma were abducted?"

Marissa nodded. "He identified himself as a police officer, but obviously he wasn't."

Dunn turned to his agents. "What have you got?"

Laird spoke. "One UNSUB, posing as law enforcement. He stopped Ms. DeSola, incapacitated her, then forcibly removed the children from the vehicle."

"How long ago?"

"One hour, maybe less."

Dunn was angry. Jordan was more than just an agent to him, and now her family was in danger. This was personal. "Tell me you have something," he said.

"Yes, sir, we do." Laird took out his cell phone, accessed his email and showed the director the video Mindy Aberfoyle had captured from her doorbell cam. He commented on the footage. "It's clear enough for us to ID him if he's in the system."

Dunn nodded. "Has an Amber Alert been issued for the children?" he asked.

"Not yet, sir."

"What the hell are you waiting for? Make the call. Get that footage out to the media now!"

"Yes, sir," the agents said. The two men wished Marissa well and took their leave.

Director Dunn turned to his friend. "It'll be all right, Marissa. We're going to find Emma and Aiden."

Marissa began to cry. "If anything has happened to them, I'll just die," she said.

"We're going to do everything we can to make sure that doesn't happen," Dunn said. He squeezed her hand. "Can you give me a minute? I need to call Jordan, bring her up to speed on the situation."

"Of course."

"I'll be right back."

Dunn stepped out of the ward, found a quiet place at the end of the hallway, then made one of the most difficult phone calls of his career.

CHAPTER 34

HALLIER CALLED AHEAD.

"Rafferty."

"It's Hallier, sergeant. Are you and your men in La Fortuna?"

"Yes, sir," the soldier replied.

"Give me a rally point."

"There's an abandoned car lot on the outskirts of town," Sergeant Rafferty replied. "Signs still up. Paloma Auto Sales. It's quiet, nondescript, out of the way. No one's going to pay attention to us. Your men can gear up there."

"Very good," Hallier replied. He checked the location with the driver, got an estimated time of arrival. "We'll be there in twenty minutes."

"Copy that, sir. What's the destination?"

"Casa de los Niños."

"The orphanage?" Rafferty asked.

"We have solid intel that puts the target there."

"Time to put the dog down, sir?"

"If we need to."

"Just give us the word," Rafferty said. "We'll bag 'em and tag 'em for you, no problem."

"Let me be clear, sergeant," Hallier said. "No one makes a move until you get my green. The primary objective is to take the target alive and return him stateside. Only if the mission goes south are you authorized to neutralize him."

"Understood, sir."

"Prepare your men. We move on my arrival at the location."

"Copy that, sir," Rafferty replied. "We'll be ready and waiting."

Hallier hung up.

Jordan felt her phone vibrate, checked the display: ANDREW DUNN. She answered the call. "Agent Quest."

"Jordan, it's Andrew Dunn."

Andrew Dunn? The director's informal introduction brought immediate cause for concern. "Yes, sir?"

"Where are you now?"

"En route to La Fortuna with Colonel Hallier and DARPA, sir."

"Can you talk privately?"

"Yes."

Dunn chose his words carefully. "Jordan, a situation has developed here. But before I get into the details, you need to know that every departmental resource is being brought to bear to rectify the matter as quickly and safely as possible."

Rectify the matter? Jordan felt her stomach drop. She wanted to be sick. She knew what the call was about. She kept her cool, lowered her voice, spoke as calmly as she could. "What's happened to my family?" she asked.

Chris heard the gut-wrenching question. He stared at her, listened intently.

184

The director continued. "Marissa has been attacked."

Jordan recalled the earlier disturbing psychic connection she had made with her housekeeper... *the man at her window... the jolt of electricity that suddenly seized her friend, rendered her unconscious...*

One of the DARPA commandos glanced at her, gave her a puzzled look. Jordan maintained her composure. Inside, she wanted to scream. The soldier turned away.

"And my children?"

Dunn paused. "They're missing, Jordan. Whoever attacked Marissa took the children."

Jesus, Jordan thought. *Stop the van! Let me out! Where are my kids? WHERE ARE MY CHILDREN? I can't be here. Not here, not now! Get me home! Oh, God!*

"We've obtained video footage of the kidnapping," Dunn said. "I'm texting it to your phone now. This is going to be hard Jordan, but you need to watch it. Tell me if you recognize the man. I'll hold."

Jordan took a deep breath, exhaled. "Okay," she replied. She braced herself before opening the text message, then watched as the dramatic event unfolded... saw Marissa's body jump as she received the shock... watched her slump in her seat... the assailant ordering her children out of the car... Aiden being shoved from behind.

The sonofabitch laid his hands on my child!

With every passing second that she watched the video Jordan was losing the internal struggle between anguished mother and emotionally controlled FBI

185

agent. She refocused, pulled herself together. Got to keep my head in the game, she thought. She returned to the directors' call.

"I've never seen him before in my life," she said.

"Are you sure?"

"Positive."

"All right," Dunn said. "I've requested the footage be run through facial recognition. If he's in the system, we'll find him."

"What about my kids?"

"A nation-wide Amber Alert has been issued. Every law enforcement agency within a five-hundred-mile radius of the abduction site has also been notified. They know they're looking for the children of an FBI agent."

"Did you ping their cellphones?"

"We did. We found Emma's in the car. She must have dropped it when he took her."

"What about Aiden's?"

"We can't locate the signal. He must have turned it off."

Jordan felt the van slow, then stop. "We're here," Hallier called out. He opened his door. "Everybody out."

"Oh, God!" Jordan said. "We're here."

"I heard," Dunn said. His voice was positive, strong. "Listen to me, Jordan. You know I mean it when I say I understand what you're going through. I went through it with my girls. If it hadn't been for you, they might be dead right now. You saved their lives. I'm telling you this as your friend first and your boss second. I won't let

186

any harm come to Aiden or Emma. There's not a rock on this planet this bastard could try to hide under that we wouldn't find him. I give you my word on that."

Jordan stepped out of the van. "Thank you, director. I know you'll do your best."

"Stay calm, Jordan," Dunn said. "As best as you can, anyway. I'll be back in touch as soon as I know more." The director ended the call.

Chris asked, "What was that about?"

Jordan quelled the rising tide of emotion once again. "Marissa has been hurt. Aiden and Emma are missing."

"What do you mean, missing?"

"Someone's taken them."

"You mean they've been *kidnapped*?"

"Yes." There were tears in her eyes.

"You have to tell Hallier," Chris said.

"I can't," Jordan said.

"Why the hell not?"

"Because he'll pull me."

"You can't be serious, Jordan!" Chris said. "With everything that's going on back home you don't really give a shit about the operation, do you?"

"I'm the only one here who doesn't want to see Commander Egan dead. Hallier may say he wants to bring him back alive, but I don't believe him for a second."

"And for good reason," Chris said. "There's never been a greater risk to national security than Egan. He's a murderer, Jordan. A stone-cold military killing machine."

"I don't believe that's true."

"Why not?"

"Everything he did was because he was *programmed* to do it. He wasn't given a choice in the matter."

"Are you saying you're seriously prepared to put your ass on the line to save this guy?"

"Isn't that why we're here?"

Hanover looked at his partner and sighed. "One of these days you're going to get us both killed."

"Maybe," Jordan said. "But it's sure as hell not going to be today."

CHAPTER 35

EGAN RECOGNIZED THE SOUND of Diego Mendoza's Hummer, peered out through the window blind in the dark room, watched as the vehicle rolled to a stop outside the main gate. He turned to Hernando. "Showtime."

"What do you want me to do?" the old man asked. He was trying to put on a brave face, but his voice deceived him. Inside, he was terrified.

Egan smiled. "First, sit down. We need to have a chat." Hernando sat on the edge of his desk in the small office.

"When this goes does, you're going to see some changes happen to me," Egan explained.

Hernando looked confused. "What kind of changes?"

"For starters, my physical appearance may become altered," the commander explained. "If that happens don't be alarmed. It's only temporary and I'm controlling it."

"Okay."

Egan continued. "Remember what happened when I helped little Teresa to breathe again? That glow you saw coming from my hands?"

Hernando nodded. "Yes."

"My abilities permit me to do much more than that.

And if I use them, you need to promise me one thing."

"Anything."

"That you'll never breathe a word of it to anyone. If anyone asks, you'll deny having seen anything at all. It's for your own safety."

Hernando was concerned. "You sound worried, Ben."

Egan shook his head. "Not for myself. I'm just concerned about you. There are people coming for me. I can feel it."

"Then leave," Hernando urged. "Run. If anyone asks, I'll tell them you were never here. I'll take care of Mendoza and his men myself."

Egan smiled. "It's not as simple as that, my friend. These are not the kind of people you can run from for very long. I knew they'd track me down eventually. It was only a matter of time. And as far as Mendoza's men are concerned, no, you can't."

"These men," Hernando said. "What will they do when they find you?"

Egan shrugged. "That's the question of the day. I'm not sure if I'm still the invaluable asset they once considered me to be. For all I know they've already deployed a new and improved version of me into the world. So, if I had to guess, I'd say they're going to kill me."

"What do you mean... asset?"

"I belong to DARPA," Egan explained. "The Defense Advanced Research Projects Agency of the United States."

"The American military think tank?" Hernando asked.

"The same," Egan replied. "I'm kind of a secret experiment that went off the rails."

"And this project gave you these powers?"

"And then some."

Hernando crossed himself. "Dios mío," he said.

"God had nothing to do with it," Egan said. "This was all manmade."

Hernando and Egan heard car doors slam outside. Mendoza and his men were making their arrival known.

A motion sensor light affixed atop a pole at the entrance to the compound flickered to life and bathed the grounds in a pale-yellow glow.

Mendoza looked up. "Take it out," he ordered.

Matias raised his weapon, shot out the light. Shards of shattered glass rained down, tinkled on the roof of the Hummer.

"Let's get this over with," Mendoza said. He issued the order. "Take them."

As several of the men climbed the fence and stood beside the woodpile in front of the gate, Egan and Hernando ran down the hall to the main entrance of the building where the car battery sat on the floor. Four lines of electrical cable leading inside from their covert burial points on the grounds, their ends stripped down to the bare copper wire, lay on the wooden floor. Egan picked up the line he needed and touched the copper wire to the battery.

The connection was made, the circuit completed.

Through the window, Hernando watched the propane cylinder hidden in the woodpile suddenly explode. A tremendous *boom!* rocked the orphanage. Three of Mendoza's men were thrown high into the air by the concussive force of the blast and landed motionless in the middle of the property.

"Cover!" Matias yelled. He threw himself on top of his boss, took him to the ground, protected him from the catastrophic explosion.

Mendoza clambered to his feet and took stock of his team. Three of his men lay on the ground. Neither offered a cry for help nor made a sound. One man had his arm ripped from his body in the unexpected blast. They were most likely dead, Diego thought. No matter. If they couldn't get back in the fight, they were of no further use to him, anyway.

Alonzo Perez's four men fell back, took cover behind their vehicles. "What are you doing?" Perez yelled. "Get in there! Find the sonofabitch! Kill him!"

Egan stared out the window, observed the human destruction the makeshift bomb had caused, calculated his next move. "What do you call three dead bad guys, Hernando?" he said.

The old man didn't answer. He stared in disbelief at the dead men laying on his property. The severity of the situation set in. They were engaged in all-out war now.

"A good start," Egan said.

Outside, Perez's men advanced into the compound. One two-man team broke right, made it to the main building, then dropped low and hugged the wall as they

192

crept toward the back door. The second team spread out. One man found cover behind the slide in the children's play area, the other the side of the work shed.

Egan knew what was coming. "Get down!" he yelled. He pulled Hernando to the floor, held him down as round after round of automatic gunfire ripped through the walls of the building. When the assault had finally ended, the old man dared to look up. When he did, he witnessed the most incredible sight. A translucent wall of pink light surrounded them. Beyond the light, dozens of spent slugs littered the floor. Not one had penetrated the spectacular force field. Suddenly the barrier consumed itself and disappeared.

"You okay?" Egan whispered.

Hernando nodded. He picked up one of the slugs. The words stumbled out of his mouth. "There was a light... the bullets, they just bounced off... how did you..."

"Like I said," Egan replied, "I've had a few upgrades." The commander peered out one of the bullet holes. The two men came out of hiding, removed their spent clips, slammed fresh magazines into the assault rifles, racked the weapons and were advancing on the building. A secondary assault was imminent. "Stay down," Egan warned.

The old man nodded.

Egan rolled across the floor, picked up one of the electrical wires, positioned it over the battery terminal, peered out a hole in the wall, waited. "Closer..." he said.

The men moved forward cautiously, then stopped

and listened.

"Come on," Egan said. "Just one more step."

One of the men looked at his partner, raised his hand, signaled his authorization to continue.

"That's good," Egan whispered. "Come to daddy, you sonofabitch."

The men raised their weapons, prepared to fire.

Egan touched the electrical lead to the car battery.

From his vantage point inside the building, Egan watched the propane tank ignite inside the van. The explosion ripped the vehicle apart, tossing it high into the air. Pieces of the rusty old vehicle whistled though the air and lodged in the supply shed wall. The force of the blast blew out the front window of the building. Egan looked outside. The would-be assassins were nowhere to be seen. They had been standing beside the van at the exact second the detonation had occurred. The weapon one of the men had been carrying lay on the ground where the van once stood. Their chance of surviving such a blast at ground zero was impossible. They were gone.

Two men remained. Egan moved to the rear door of the building, listened.

Bullets shot from the high-powered weapons of the two-man assault team had tore clean through the wooden structure and left splintered holes in the back walls.

Egan heard moaning sounds, coming from outside. He raised his hand, activated Channeler. The back wall reflected the rose-red glow emanating from his palms.

He threw open the door.

The two men lay on the ground, victims of friendly fire. The assailants had underestimated the power of the M-16's. The rounds had traveled through the building and out the back wall, striking and wounding the second assault team.

Egan stepped outside. As one of the men raised his weapon the second tried to crawl away. Egan pulled the gun from his hands. "You two don't get off that easy," he said. He shot each man in the head, threw the weapon on the ground, then stepped back inside to check on Hernando.

"I heard gunfire," Hernando said. "Are you okay?"

"Fine," Egan replied. "I'm bulletproof, remember?"

"About that," Hernando said. "How did you…?"

From outside came the crack of a gunshot.

Egan watched his friend crumple to the floor.

Hernando had been hit.

CHAPTER 36

HAVING REACHED the San Gabriel Mountain region, Elton Mannafort drove the police sedan off the highway and followed the bumpy road to his cabin deep in the woods, avoiding teeth-chattering potholes and negotiating half a dozen blind turns along the way. This part of the region lacked the cover of tall trees. Instead, chaparral and other dense shrubs, as well as alder and cottonwood trees, provided vegetation. Elton parked the car under the canopy of a drooping willow.

He looked over his shoulder, called back to the children. "We're here."

Aiden shifted in his seat and felt his cellphone in his back pocket. Many times on the drive he'd wanted to take it out, turn it on and try to contact his mother, but the creep glanced frequently in his rear-view mirror, checking on them.

Now was the time. As the man fiddled with his car keys and collected his satchel from the passenger seat, Aiden slipped the phone out of his pocket, turned the ring switch to vibrate mode, and powered up the device. The screen glowed. Aiden pulled up his pant leg, shoved the phone deep into his sock, then sat up straight as the man exited the car and opened his door.

"Get out," he said.

"I don't feel well," Emma complained.

"You're fine."

"She's not fine, asshole," Aiden retorted. "My sister gets sick on long drives, always has. Mom gives her Dramamine. But you wouldn't know that because you're a fucking idiot."

"She'll feel better once she gets a couple deep breaths of clean mountain air into her lungs." He pointed to the cabin. "Enough complaining. Out of the car, now."

Aiden stepped out. Mannafort grabbed him by the collar. "Listen to me," he said. "You run and she dies. Got it?"

"Touch her and I'll kill you," Aiden warned.

Mannafort had had enough of the insolent youth. He threw him to the ground, raised his foot to kick him, held back. "You're really starting to get on my nerves, kid."

Aiden had landed hard on the ground. He spat dirt out of his mouth, pulled himself up and stared at the creep. He smiled. "I have that effect on some people," he replied. "They're usually assholes who bear a striking resemblance to you."

"Little shit," Mannafort repeated. He walked around the car, dragged Emma out of the back seat, hauled her to her brother's side.

"You okay, Em?" Aiden asked. He put his arm around his sister.

Emma nodded. "I think so."

"Family reunion's over," Mannafort said. "Up the hill. March."

Aiden took his sister's hand, helped her over the rocky terrain. "What are you going to do to us?" Emma asked.

"What do you think?" Mannafort said.

"Don't listen to him, Emma," Aiden said. "He's just trying to scare you."

"I am scared."

"Don't be," Aiden said.

Mannafort shoved Aiden, tried to make him fall. "What are you going to do?" he asked. "Be a hero? Save the day?"

Aiden was two-steps ahead of his captor up the steep incline which led to the cabin. He acted quickly, used the elevation to his advantage. "That's exactly what I was thinking," he replied.

Faster than Elton could react, Aiden turned and shot his leg back with all his might. The karate kick caught Mannafort square in his face. He screamed in agony. The man brought his hands to his face, tried to stem the flow of blood gushing from his nose. Aiden jumped again, following the first well-placed kick with a second straight to the middle of Mannafort's chest. The crushing contact to his solar plexus took the air out of Elton's lungs. He dropped to his knees.

Aiden grabbed his sister by the hand. "Run, Emma!" he yelled. *"Run!"*

Mannafort struggled to his feet, slowly regained his senses, and watched the children as they ran over the crest of the hill towards the cabin. "There's nowhere to go!" he yelled. He hurried up the trail and over the hill, pulled the stun stick from the small of his back, powered up the weapon, held it at his side.

Ahead, the children had stopped. Emma had finally succumbed to car sickness. Aiden stood beside her while the poor girl wrenched into the tall grass.

Elton pointed the stun stick at Aiden. "That was a very stupid thing to do," he said.

Aiden stood in front of his sister. "How's the nose?" he asked, pleased with himself at the effectiveness of the kick. "Looks pretty fucked up to me."

"Not half as much as you'll be if you ever try a stunt like that again," Elton replied. He waved the stun stick in the cabin's direction. "Door's open. Make yourself at home."

Aiden tended to his sister. "You all right, Em?"

Emma stood up, wiped her face. She nodded. "Better."

"Good."

Aiden realized the opportunity for escape had been lost. He took Emma by the hand. "C'mon," he said. "Better do what he says."

The children walked ahead, entered the cabin.

Elton followed, then closed and locked the door.

∞ ∞ ∞

At FBI headquarters in downtown Los Angeles, Technical Specialist Karen Wentworth had been assigned to the rapidly assembled Quest task force and was monitoring Aiden's cell signal when suddenly a location blip appeared on her computer screen. She called out to the team, "Got him!"

The agent's gathered around the monitor. Karen picked up the phone, placed a call.

"Dunn."

"We have him, Director," Karen said. "Aiden's phone just came online."

"Where is he?"

"The cell signal puts him in the San Gabriel Mountains."

"I'm scrambling HRT," Dunn said. "You'll be liaising with them. Give them everything you've got on the boy's location."

"Copy that, sir."

Dunn made the call to the Hostage Rescue Team. Commander Tom Gibson and his team had been placed on standby and were awaiting his call. "We have a location," the director said. "San Gabriel Mountains. GPS coordinates are on their way to you now."

"Copy that, sir," Gibson replied. "Consider us in the air."

CHAPTER 37

"HERNANDO!" EGAN YELLED. He ran to the old man's aid, dropped to the floor. "Where are you hit?"

Hernando glanced down at his right shoulder. "There," he said. The blood had begun to seep out of the wound, dampen his shirt.

Egan helped him up from the ground, shuffled him across the room to cover. Hernando sat down in the corner. He lifted the old man's hand to his shoulder, placed it on the wound. "Keep pressure on it," he said, then stood. "Wait here."

Hernando heard the anger in the commander's voice. "Where are you going?" he asked.

"To finish this," Egan replied. He had activated Channeler. His palms glowed bright red.

Outside, Egan heard the screech of brakes. Men were yelling. He recognized the well-practiced tone of comply-or-die commands being issued. "Drop your weapons! Get on the ground! Do it now!" A volley of gunfire followed, then silence.

A familiar voice called out. "Commander Egan, this is Colonel Quentin Hallier. Come out of the building now. Place your hands above your head and interlock your fingers."

From the doorway Egan looked across the room. Hernando grimaced. The old man was in a great deal of pain.

"Is that who I think it is?" Hernando asked.

Egan nodded.

"They've come for you?"

"Yes."

"What are you going to do?"

"I'm not sure yet."

"You said they'd kill you if ever they found you."

"Probably."

"You can't let that happen, Ben. Not after all we've been through together."

"It's not my decision, Hernando," Egan replied. "I've been responsible for a lot of deaths. Maybe this is how it ends."

"The people you killed. Why did you do it?"

"I was under orders."

"Then you didn't have a choice in the matter, did you?"

"It doesn't matter."

"Yes, it does," Hernando said. "A murderer kills for the thrill of killing. A soldier kills out of duty to country. There's a huge difference."

Hallier yelled again. "There's no reason to put more civilian lives at risk, commander. Don't make us have to take the building by force."

Egan cracked open the door, peered outside.

"Don't do it, Ben," Hernando said.

Thins beams of red light broke through the gap in the door and pierced the darkness of the room. Lasers, from high-powered weapons. The DARPA commandos had acquired their target.

Egan called out. "I have a man in here who's been shot. He requires medical attention. You treat him first."

"That can be arranged," Hallier replied. "Stand by. I'm sending someone in."

"I want the agent," Egan said.

Hallier paused. "Who?"

"Don't screw with me, Colonel. You know exactly who I'm talking about. Send in Agent Quest. Have her bring a medical kit. After this man's injury has been dealt with, we'll discuss the terms of my surrender."

Jordan ran to the van, grabbed the field medical kit, returned. Hallier stopped her, shook his head. "Not happening," he said.

"You heard what the commander said," Jordan replied. "He wants me."

"It's too dangerous."

"Sir, I've got this. Besides, you brought me here to help."

"I brought you here to help us locate Commander Egan," Hallier retorted. "You've done that. This is out of your depth."

"Do you want the commander back or not?" Jordan asked.

"The answer to that question is obvious, Agent Quest."

"That's right. So, whether you like it or not, it's on me to make that happen." Jordan walked into the compound.

"You have five minutes," Hallier called out.

"I'll take as much time as I need," Jordan called back. "Tell your men to stand down. No one makes a move until you see me walk out the door with Commander Egan!"

Hallier waved to his men, instructed them to lower their weapons. "That woman is stubborn as hell," he muttered to himself.

Chris was standing beside him, heard the comment. "You have no idea," he said.

Jordan reached the front steps of the main building.

"Hands," Egan said.

Jordan raised her arms.

"Turn."

Jordan did as he instructed.

Egan removed her firearm, opened the door. "Get inside."

Jordan entered the room, saw the man lying in the corner of the room. She walked over to Hernando. "How bad is he hurt?" she asked.

"Looks like a through and through," Egan replied.

Jordan gingerly removed Hernando's shirt, inspected the wound. The blood stuck to the cotton fabric. The old man gritted his teeth as Jordan pulled the wet cloth away from his skin. "You're right," she said. "There's an exit wound." She opened the medical kit, removed the required supplies and began to treat the gunshot.

"How long have you had it?" Egan asked as he watched her work.

"What are you talking about?"

"Your gift."

Jordan wiped away the blood at the entry and exit points of the wound. "All my life," she replied.

"It's powerful," Egan said. "You got into my head. That's not an easy thing to do."

Jordan applied a thin pressure dressing to the wound, carefully wrapped Hernando's arm in gauze, taped it in place. "Not nearly as powerful as what I saw you do at the Pyramid," she replied. "How was that possible?"

Egan cracked open the door, looked out. The commandos were keeping their distance. "Sorry, that's top secret."

"Considering the situation we find ourselves in," Jordan said, "I'm thinking your days of keeping national security secrets are pretty much over, wouldn't you say?"

"I guess I'd have to agree with that."

"Can you do it whenever you want to?"

"Do what?"

"You know... *travel*."

"You mean teleport."

"Yes."

Egan nodded. "I suppose so."

"Is that how you got here?"

"Yes."

"When I connected with you psychically and saw you on the trail, and you spoke to me, were you already here?"

"I was."

"That's incredible."

Egan smiled. "I'm a pretty incredible guy, in general."

"Could you do it again?" Jordan asked.

"You mean teleport?"

"Yes."

"I suppose so."

"You should know they've brought a weapon."

"What do you mean?"

"Hallier alluded to it," Jordan explained. "He wouldn't say specifically what it could do, but my guess is it's been designed to reverse the effect of whatever they exposed you to and return you to normal."

"So much for having superpowers," Egan quipped. "It was fun while it lasted."

Jordan turned her attention back to Hernando. "How are you feeling, sir?" she asked.

"Better." The old man held her hand. "Thank you."

"You're welcome."

Hernando maintained his grip on her hand. "Please don't let them hurt Ben," he said. "If it wasn't for him, my kids might be dead by now."

"Your kids?" Jordan asked.

"The orphans we care for here," Hernando explained. "Nine precious little lives. Those men your team shot outside had come here to kill us. If they'd succeeded there is absolutely no doubt in my mind, they'd have eventually killed the children too. He's saved all our lives."

Jordan looked at Egan. "You did that? You saved the kids?"

Egan shrugged. "I was in the right place at the right time," he replied. "It was no big deal."

"It's a *very* big deal," Hernando stated.

Jordan turned away. She looked upset.

"What's wrong?" Egan asked.

Jordan gathered her courage. "I'm going to ask you to do something for me," she said. "And if you agree I'm probably going to go to prison for the rest of my life."

"I'm listening," Egan said.

"I need your help."

"For what?"

"To save my children."

CHAPTER 38

IN THE LIVING ROOM of the mountain cabin, Elton Mannafort paced back and forth, talking to himself. The wooden floorboards of the old place showed their age and creaked beneath his feet.

"You brought them here, to the cabin?"

"Why not?

"What were you thinking?"

"It doesn't matter."

"The hell it doesn't!"

"You're overreacting again. Like you always do."

"I've got two words for you that says I'm not: Carrie Schumacher."

"My point exactly."

"What's that supposed to mean?"

"When the bitch finds her dead kid's, I *want* her to make the connection."

"What if she leads them to the others?"

"There's nothing to connect them to us."

Elton pointed to the window. "You've buried ten bodies out there!"

"So? The cops don't suspect us. If they did, they'd have torn this mountain apart looking for them."

Elton shook his head. "I don't like this."

"You don't have to. I'm in charge."

"You've pushed it too far this time. You shouldn't

have taken her kids."

"Meddlesome bitch has no one to blame but herself."

"You'll get us both caught. And you know what'll happen then!"

"We won't get the needle."

"Needle, life… what difference does it make?"

"Stop your whining."

"You're not listening to reason."

"Shut up and get the shovel."

"This is wrong."

"Am I going to have to do this on my own?"

"No."

"Then check on the brats. Hurry. I want to be out of here in an hour."

Elton opened the bedroom door. Aiden lay on one of the two beds in the small room, Emma on the other. He had secured the wrists and ankles of both children with plastic zip ties. Black cloth hoods covered their heads.

Aiden heard the door creak. He raised his head, looked in the sound's direction. "How's the nose, asshole?" he said.

Elton disregarded the barb. "Which one first?" he said.

"The boy. Little prick's getting on my last nerve."

"I still don't like this."

"You don't have to like it. You just have to do it."

Aiden piped up. "Still talking to yourself, freak?"

"Don't listen to him."

"You'd better listen to me, nutbar," Aiden said. "You're done. Cops will be here any minute."

"What's he talking about?"

"Nothing."

"Oh, yeah?" Aiden said. "You ever heard of cellular triangulation?"

"Get him on his feet."

Elton grabbed the boy by his arm, hauled him off the bed, propped him against the wall. Feet bound, Aiden struggled to keep his balance.

"It's how a cell phone signal can be tracked by measuring its distance from the three nearest towers," Aiden said.

"We'll deal with him first, then come back for the girl."

Aiden pressed. "You never thought to check me for a cellphone, did you Sherlock?"

Concerned, Elton spoke to himself. "Well, did you?"

"What?"

"Check him for a phone?"

"No."

"Why the hell not?"

"That doesn't matter much now."

"So, the kid's right?"

"Who gives a shit? We're in the mountains. Cellular reception is spotty at the best of times."

"That's not the point."

"Pat him down."

"What?"

"See if he's telling the truth."

Elton checked Aiden's pockets. No phone. "Nothing. Happy now?"

"Check him again."

"He's clean."

"Do it."

"He's just trying to scare you."

"Humor me."

Elton ran his hands across Aiden's arms and legs. In his sock he found the phone. "You little bastard!" he yelled.

"Dumbass," Aiden said. The boy sounded pleased with himself. Elton could tell that under the cloth hood he was smiling.

"He's right. The cops are coming!"

"Won't matter."

"Why not?"

"By the time they get here they'll both be dead."

Aiden spoke. "We'd been traveling for an hour. You seriously think finding my phone now will make any difference? If you had an ounce of intelligence, you'd drop us somewhere and high-tail it out of here while you still can."

"He's right. We need to leave."

"Not until we finish what we started." Elton grabbed Aiden by the arm. "Let's go."

"Fuck you!" Aiden yelled.

Elton dragged him across the bedroom floor.

"Aiden," she called out. "Where are you? Aiden? *AIDEN!*"

∞ ∞ ∞

Now airborne, the FBI Blackhawk helicopter set

course for the San Gabriel Mountains.

The pilot watched the blip identifying the location of Aiden's cellphone flash on the screen. "GPS signal is solid, sir," the pilot said.

"What's our time to target?"

"Seven minutes."

"Think you can push this bird any faster?"

The pilot nodded. "Yes, sir."

"Do it."

CHAPTER 39

JORDAN SHARED THE CRUSHING NEWS with Egan. "My children are missing," she said. "They've been kidnapped."

"Good God," Egan replied.

Hearing herself say the words, Jordan didn't know what she wanted to do first, scream or cry. What she knew was that this was not the time to break down. She held back the tears, fought hard to keep herself in check.

Egan could hear the emotional conflict in her voice, the inner turmoil that was wearing her down, tearing her apart. Like the plight of the children of Casa de los Niños, who in their altogether brief lives had already suffered too much loss, the thought of a family being ripped apart by a human predator filled him with rage.

"Why are you here?" Egan asked. "Shouldn't you be in the States trying to find your kids?"

"It just happened."

"When?"

"A couple of hours ago."

"What has the FBI told you? Do they know who took them?"

"They're working on it now."

"Why your kids?"

"What do you mean?"

"Why were they targeted?"

"I honestly have no idea," Jordan said. "My work, perhaps."

"Sounds like you need to find a new line of work."

"What I need to *find* are my kids."

Hernando spoke. "I've seen what you can do, Ben. Can you help her?"

Jordan stared at Egan. The look of desperation in her eyes was too much for him to bear.

Egan nodded. "What do you want me to do?"

"Us."

"Excuse me?"

"What I want *us* to do," Jordan said. "I want you to use your abilities to take me to my children."

"You mean teleport?"

"Yes."

Egan shook his head. "I'm not so sure about that."

"What do you mean?" Jordan asked.

"I've only done it once, from the Pyramid to here."

"That doesn't mean you can't do it again."

"That's true," Egan replied. "But it's only been me that's traveled. I've taken no one with me before. I don't know if that's even possible."

"You have to try."

Egan walked around the room. "What if it goes wrong?" he said. "I have no idea what could happen to you. You could die."

"He's going to kill my children," Jordan pleaded. "If it means saving their lives, I'm willing to take that chance."

"This is nuts," Egan said.

Jordan looked outside. The DARPA commandos were holding their positions. She turned to Egan. "You're my only hope, commander. Will you help me? Please?"

Egan sighed. "All right," he said. "How do you propose we do this?"

"We merge our abilities," Jordan said. "I can see where my children are, but I can't get to them. You can. You lock on to my thoughts and we travel. You take us there."

"That could work."

"It has to work."

"What happens when we get there?"

"I'll eliminate the threat," Jordan said. "When my kids are safe, we'll come back, right here, to this exact location. No one will ever know we've left. We'll have only been gone for a matter of minutes."

"What's stopping me from not coming back?" Egan asked.

Jordan shrugged. "Other than giving me your word that you won't, nothing at all."

Egan looked at Hernando. "How's the shoulder doing?"

"Why are you worried about my shoulder?" the old man said. "The lady's asking you for help. What are you waiting for?"

Egan smiled at his friend. "Remember the stuff I did earlier, helping Teresa… moving the woodpile?"

"Yes," Hernando replied.

"You ain't seen nothin' yet." He turned to Jordan.

"Okay, I'll do it."

Jordan smiled. "Thank you, Commander."

"You can thank me when I get us back here in one piece," Egan said.

"I'll need my weapon," Jordan said.

Egan handed her the gun. "Now give me your hands," he said.

Jordan placed her hands in his.

"You ready?" Egan asked.

"As I'll ever be."

Egan joked. "From Costa Rica to the USA and back. Just imagine the Air Miles you could have racked up."

Jordan closed her eyes, concentrated on her children, focused on their vital force, connected with their energy. She squeezed the commander's hands. "Got it?"

Egan read her mind. "Here we go," he said.

Hernando watched Egan's hands glow rose-red. A strange energy filled the room. Hernando felt it pass through his body, as though the air in the room had suddenly been replaced with a field of static electricity. The hairs on his arms rose.

A fraction of a second later the commander and the FBI agent were ensconced in a shape-shifting field of brilliant pink light.

A sudden, brilliant flash caused Hernando to look away from the miraculous sight.

When he turned back, they were gone.

He knew he had just witnessed the impossible.

The old man crossed himself, looked toward the Heavens. "Dios mío," he said.

CHAPTER 40

FBI CHOPPER PILOT STU WASSERMANN spoke to Commander Gibson as the team flew over Big Santa Anita Canyon. "GPS puts the boy's phone somewhere in this vicinity," he said. He looked down through the helicopter window at the forest canopy below. "Tree cover's too thick, sir. There's nowhere to land. Your men will have to follow the signal on foot."

Gibson nodded. "How close can you get us to the target?" he asked.

Wassermann motioned over his shoulder. "We passed a small clearing a half mile back," the pilot said. "I should have enough room to put her down there."

"Do it," Gibson said.

Wassermann had just started to bank the helicopter when suddenly he stopped the bird, hovered. "Oh, shit," he said.

"What is it?" Gibson asked.

"The screen. Look!"

The flashing blue dot on the GPS monitoring screen had vanished.

"We've lost the signal," Wassermann said.

"Sonofabitch," Gibson said. He called back to his team. "I need a location marker. Drop smoke now!"

Agent Shelby reached for a smoke grenade, pulled the pin, tossed it from the helicopter, watched it disappear through the trees. "Smoke's away, sir," he said.

Lazy wisps of yellow smoke slowly drifted up through the treetops. "Location's marked," Shelby yelled.

"Copy that," Gibson said. To Wassermann he said, "Get us to that clearing."

"Yes, sir."

The chopper banked hard to the left, picked up speed. The pilot found the location, circled the bird. "Hold tight," he said.

The Blackhawk descended quickly, touched down featherlight.

The agents jumped out of the aircraft, rallied at the edge of the clearing.

In the distance, the smoke stood out against the twilight sky.

"We're losing light," Gibson said. "Step it up, double time."

The Hostage Rescue Team ran into the dark forest in search of the missing children.

CHAPTER 41

HAVING POWERED OFF the cellphone, Elton threw it against the wooden cabin wall, smashing the device into pieces. Feet bound by the zip ties, unable to walk, Aiden struggled, trying helplessly to stop himself from being dragged across the bedroom floor. "It's all right, Emma!" he called out. "Don't worry! I'll be back for you!"

"I wouldn't count on that," Elton said. He opened the bedroom door, hauled the boy into the hallway, then halted. A high-pitched whining sound, followed immediately by a brilliant flash of pink light, caught his attention. He had owned the cabin for years, been here a hundred times, knew every squeak, pop, creak and moan it made. But he had never heard this sound before or seen this strange light. It was emanating from the living room.

Elton kept many weapons hidden around the home in the event of an emergency. Here in the hallway, behind a framed portrait of Big Sur, a Walther PPK handgun had been secretly stored. He had secured the top of the picture frame to the wall using a piano hinge. Elton raised the picture, removed the weapon, chambered a round, and lowered the picture back into place. He continued along the hallway, stepped around the corner, then froze.

A man and a woman were standing in the middle of the cabin. The woman drew her gun and pointed it at him. She wore a bulletproof vest. The nameplate across the chest read 'FBI.'

Elton panicked. "Who are you?" he yelled. "Where did you come from? How did you get in here?"

Aiden struggled against his captor, tried to break free. Elton pulled him closer, placed the gun against the boy's head.

Jordan took a step forward. "Let go of my son!" she yelled.

Elton recognized Jordan. "It's you," he said.

Unable to see through the cloth hood, Aiden heard his mother's voice. "Mom?" he asked. "Is that you?"

"Yes, baby," Jordan replied. "It's me. Stay still, Aiden. Don't move."

The man standing beside the FBI agent spoke next. "Let the boy go," he demanded.

Be brave, Elton thought. Don't let them see you're afraid. "Or what?" he yelled. "You going to shoot me? Try. I'll blow the kid's brains clear across the room. You really want to take that chance?"

"No," Egan replied calmly. "We definitely don't want to see that happen. To tell you the truth, we were kind of hoping you'd just give yourself up. We're on a bit of a deadline."

Elton stared at Egan. He couldn't believe the man's matter-of-fact reply. "Are you crazy?" he asked.

"Not at all," Egan said. "I'm quite sane. You I'm not so sure about."

Elton acknowledged the identification on Jordan's vest. "She's FBI," he said. "What are you?"

Egan smiled. "Well, my birthday's in October, so I guess that makes me a Libra."

Jordan took another step forward, trying to close the distance between her and the gunman and better her chance for a clean headshot. "Who are you? What do you want with my children?"

"You ruined everything," Elton said. "She should have been mine. Just like all the others."

Jordan looked confused. "Who should have been yours?"

"Carrie Schumacher."

Carrie Schumacher, Jordan thought. The young mother who had been abducted from the grocery store parking lot. Jordan recalled the case. She wasn't even officially part of the investigation. She had been enjoying lunch with a friend, Detective Catherine Juhasz of the City of Pomona police department when the call came in. A hiker on a trail in the San Gabriel Mountains had reported passing someone who matched the description of the missing woman. When Catherine apologized for having to cut their time short to follow up on the lead, Jordan offered to help, and Catherine happily accepted. At the police station, Catherine presented Jordan with the only evidence they had recovered at the scene: a cloth shopping bag, found in the Foodmart parking lot, which contained a credit card receipt bearing Carrie's name and dated on the day of her reported abduction. Jordan examined the bag and the receipt, connected with the woman's energy signature, and told Catherine everything she had seen during the moment of her psychic connection: Carrie's assault, the assailant's van, passing the hiker on the trail, the cabin in the woods. An arrest was made the following day. She recalled the accused's name.

"You're Elton Mannafort," Jordan said.

Elton beamed. "You know me."

Elton's multiple personality interjected. "I told you this was a bad idea."

"Hardly. Who's got her kid?"

"There's two of them and only one of you. You don't stand a chance."

"She knows if she tries anything the little shit is dead."

"Maybe they're not alone."

"What do you mean?"

"Maybe there are more cops outside, got the place surrounded."

"They'd have made a move by now."

"You don't know that for sure."

"I'll tell you what I do know."

"What's that?"

"None of them are leaving here alive."

Egan spoke. "I really hate to break up your riveting conversation… or whatever the hell this is… but can we get back to why we're all here? You need to let the kids go."

"Not going to happen," Elton replied.

"I beg to differ."

Elton smiled, looked at Jordan. "Say goodbye to the little prick."

Jordan screamed. "*No!*"

"I don't think so," Egan said. He raised his hand.

Elton pulled the trigger… or tried to. He stared at the weapon. His hand and finger were paralyzed, locked in position around the gun. He looked up at Egan.

The palm of the man's hand glowed rose-red. The same strange pink light he had seen emanating from the living room before he had entered the room with the boy now surrounded him.

"What's the hell?" Elton said.

"Get your son, Agent Quest," Egan said. "I'll deal with this."

Jordan stepped forward, pulled Aiden safely away from the madman. She yanked the hood off his head. "Are you okay, honey?" she asked.

"Yeah, Mom," Aiden replied. "I'm good."

"Where is your sister?"

Aiden pointed down the hall. "Back there. In the bedroom."

Jordan's eyes never left Elton. She kept her weapon trained on the man. "On my belt, Aiden," she said. "The pocketknife. You see it?"

"Yes."

"Take it out. Open the blade. Hand it to me."

Aiden did as he was told.

Jordan took the knife in one hand and cut away the zip cuff that bound her son's wrists. The nylon restraint fell to the floor. She handed the knife to the boy. "Get your feet, honey."

Aiden took the knife, released himself.

"Did he do this to your sister, too?" Jordan asked.

Aiden nodded. "Yeah, Mom."

Fueled by hatred, Jordan could feel the heat in her face. Her blood pressure was through the roof. Her hands shook. She clamped both hands around the weapon, stepped forward, steadied herself, then pressed the muzzle of her gun against Elton's temple. "Go free your sister," Jordan said. "Close the door and stay in the room. Under no circumstances do you come out until I come for you. Do you understand me?"

"Yes, Mom," the boy said.

"Good. Now go."

Aiden hesitated at first. He stared at Egan, mesmerized, his brain trying to find a logical reason for the incredible sight, couldn't. The man *glowed*.

"It's all right, son," Egan said. "Listen to your mother. Everything's fine now. Go take care of your sister. We've got this."

"Y-yes, sir," Aiden replied. He left the room, ran down the hall. Jordan heard the door close.

Egan spoke. "Put down the gun down, Agent."

Jordan's palms were damp with sweat. She gripped the gun tighter, forced the muzzle harder against Elton's head, watched him wince in pain as he turned away. With Aiden out of the room and her children now safe, a tsunami of anger came over her. The desire for vengeance was overpowering, too much to bear. She was losing her battle with self-control. "You took my kids," she said.

Egan watched her carefully. "Don't do it," he warned. "He's not worth it."

"You attacked you Marissa," Jordan said.

"Stand down, Agent," Egan said.

"Bound my children like animals. You sick, psychopathic, waste of skin."

Elton pushed back against the weapon, stared at Jordan. He smiled. "I've never done kids before," he said. "Yours would have been fun."

Jordan screamed. As she pulled the trigger, she felt her arm being pulled away. Egan used his abilities to direct the weapon away from Mannafort's head. The gunshot reported off the cabin walls.

Jordan stared vacantly at the commander. Emotionally drained, her hand fell weakly to her side.

Egan took the gun out of her hand, holstered it for her. "Go get your kids," he said quietly.

Jordan fought back the tears.

"It's all right," Egan said. "I've got this."

Jordan said nothing. She turned and walked down the hallway.

"Agent Quest," Egan called out.

Jordan turned back, stared at the DARPA soldier. "Yes?"

"Cover the children's ears."

Jordan looked at Elton Mannafort. He was no longer smiling.

She nodded. "Thank you."

"Don't mention it."

Jordan entered the room, closed the door.

Egan turned to Elton. He pointed to a chair in the corner of the room. "Take a seat," he said.

Elton looked down at the gun in his hand, then at Egan.

Egan surmised his intention. "You could try," he said, "but I'm pretty sure that wouldn't end very well for you."

Elton smiled. He held out his hand. He had intended to drop the weapon to the floor, realized he couldn't. The weapon was stuck in his grip.

"The chair," Egan said.

Elton walked across the room, sat in the chair. "Exactly what are you planning to—"

Egan raised his hand, pointed his palm at the man. "Bye bye," he said.

His body no longer under his control, Elton fought unsuccessfully against the incredible energy force that had taken over his body. He watched in horror as his hand raised on its own and placed the muzzle of the Walther PPK under his chin. "No!" he cried. "*No! No! No!*" He felt the pressure of the weapon against his skin as the gun forced his head back. Elton screamed as he watched his finger pull the trigger.

Bang!

The dead man slumped down in the chair, gun in hand, eyes staring at the floor.

Egan walked to the bedroom, knocked on the door. "Can I come in?"

"Yes?" Jordan replied.

"You guys okay?"

"We are."

Egan entered the room. "It's over," he said.

Outside in the woods, Egan heard the crack of dry twigs. He parted the dusty drape, looked out the window. "Good guys are here," he announced. "We have to go."

Emma looked up at her mother. She was about to cry.

Jordan rallied her children. "Listen to me," she said. Aiden put his arm around his sister. Emma sniffled, stopped crying. "This man and I have to go. You guys will have to stay here. But it'll just be for a minute, I promise."

Egan checked the forest again. "Six-man team, closing fast," he said anxiously. "Now would be a real good time to zap our butts out of here Agent Quest, if you catch my drift."

"I can't explain what's going on right now," Jordan said to her children. "But you cannot, under *any* circumstances, tell the police we were here."

"But that doesn't make any sense," Aiden said. "You *are* the police."

"Please, guys," Jordan pleaded. "Just trust me on this, okay? Not a single word."

The children nodded. "Okay," they said.

"I'll be home tomorrow," Jordan said. "I love you both. Now stay in the room and don't leave. The police will be here any second."

"Love you too, Mom," the children answered.

Jordan and Egan rushed out of the bedroom.

"Hurry!" Egan said.

Footsteps on the landing.

"Take my hand!" Egan said.

Jordan held tight.

"Ready?"

"Ready."

A flash of pink light lit up the room.

The cabin door crashed open. "FBI!" the agents yelled.

As the Hostage Rescue Team swarmed the small building, Agent Shelby called out. "We have the children, Commander. They're fine."

Gibson saw the dead body sitting in the chair. "Elton Mannafort, I presume," he said. He instructed his men. "UNSUB's dead. Get the children out of here. I don't want them to see this."

"Copy that," Shelby replied.

Gibson looked at the gun in Elton Mannafort's hand and shook his head. He assessed the scene for what it appeared to be. "Suicide," he said. "Too bad. I'd have preferred to put the bullet in your head myself."

CHAPTER 42

IN THE MIDDLE OF THE ROOM, pink sparks shimmered and danced in the darkness, followed by a brilliant flash of light. Hernando looked away, shielded his eyes from the incredible spectacle.

Minutes after they had disappeared, Commander Egan and the FBI agent had teleported back to the orphanage.

The return trip had left Jordan a little shaky. She teetered. Egan held her arm, steadied her. "You okay?" he asked.

Jordan nodded. "I think so."

"Hell of a trip, huh?"

"You're telling me."

Egan teased. "I have a suggestion if you're up for it."

"What's that?" Jordan asked.

"Ever been to China?"

"No. Why?"

"Let's take a stroll along the Great Wall. We could be there in seconds. Unless you'd prefer to go somewhere else."

Jordan smiled. "Very funny, Commander. I think my atoms have been jostled around enough for one lifetime."

Egan let go of her arm. "Hey, you can't blame a guy for trying."

"Thank you," Jordan said.

"For?"

"What you did back there."

Egan shrugged. "You were prepared to kill him. I couldn't allow you to carry that on your conscience for the rest of your life."

Jordan nodded. "I would have shot him if you hadn't stopped me."

"He's a predator," Egan said. "He got what he had coming to him."

"Ex-predator now."

Egan nodded. "As long as your children never tell anyone what they saw, Mannafort's death will be written up as a suicide. No one will be any the wiser."

"Don't worry," Jordan said. "They won't."

"Good," Egan said. "By the way, Aiden seems like a great kid. He handled himself exceptionally well under very difficult circumstances."

"He is. They both are."

Egan smiled. "You know, had the situation been different, I think you and I could have been great friends."

"Who says we can't be?" Jordan replied.

Egan walked to the window, looked outside. "They do," he said. The DARPA commandos had seen the flash of light inside the building. They were advancing from their positions.

"There is that little matter we have to deal with however," Jordan said.

"My surrender."

Jordan nodded. "I'm afraid so."

Hernando had been sitting quietly in the corner listening to the conversation. He spoke. "Hi Hernando. Hi Ben. How's the shoulder? It hurts like hell, but thanks for asking. You need anything? No, I'm good."

Egan laughed. "Sorry, my friend. I didn't mean to ignore you."

Jordan walked over to the old man, kneeled, checked the wound. "How are you feeling, sir?" she asked.

"I won't be playing catch with the kids for a while, but I'll survive," Hernando answered.

Jordan helped him to his feet.

From outside, Hallier's voice boomed. "Last chance, Commander!"

"It's time," Jordan said.

"Yeah, I know."

"You're surrendering on your own accord, Commander. Everything's going to be fine."

Egan walked to the door. "You better walk me out," he said.

"My pleasure," Jordan said. She joined him in the doorway.

"If you think you're leaving without me you've got another thing coming," Hernando said. He shuffled over, joined them. "Thank you, my friend," he said. "Marcella, the children and I owe you everything."

"Just take care of one another," Egan replied. "That's payment enough for me."

"Ready?" Jordan asked.

Egan took a deep breath. "Ready."

Jordan opened the door.

Egan looked down. Red dots from the DARPA commando's weapons floated across his chest. The laser lights had acquired their target.

The trio stepped out the door onto the front steps of the building.

Hallier called out, "On your knees!"

Egan complied. The commandos moved in.

"Easy," Jordan said. She watched the DARPA team take their prisoner into custody. "He's not resisting."

Hallier stepped forward. In his hand he carried a small aluminum case.

"That a present for me?" Egan asked. "Really, you shouldn't have."

Hallier opened the case and removed a small metal canister. The device resembled a smoke grenade.

"What's that?" Egan asked.

Hallier removed the safety pin, released the trigger. A clear gas escaped from the canister's nozzle.

Egan suddenly felt different, weaker.

"The antidote," Hallier replied. "It reverses the effects of your artificial augmentation."

Egan felt light-headed, woozy. "Damn, that's good stuff," he said. He was having difficulty standing.

"Take him to the truck," Hallier ordered. "Call for an extraction."

The commandos assisted Egan as he shuffled across the compound. "Wait," he said.

The commandos stopped, held fast to their prisoner.

Egan looked back at Hernando. "Go to the daycare

and get your kids, my friend," he said. "Give little Teresa a hug for me."

Hernando smiled. "I will."

"And don't come back," Egan warned. "It's not safe for you here anymore. Go to the church in San Jose. Start over."

Hernando nodded. "We will."

"Good enough," Egan said. Satisfied, he turned to the DARPA commandos. "All right, boys. Move out."

As the team headed to the truck Jordan's phone rang. She took the call. "Hello?"

"Jordan, it's Andrew Dunn. I have good news."

Jordan smiled. She knew what the director was about to say. "Yes, sir?"

"We've neutralized the threat. Aiden and Emma are safe."

"Thank God," Jordan replied. She choked back her tears. Her emotional response to the director's news was real enough. The thought of losing her children, coupled with the events of the last few hours, had been oppressively hard on her.

"HRT is bringing them back to L.A. now," Dunn said. "I'll make sure they're there to greet you when you arrive home."

"Thank you, Director," Jordan replied. "I'd really appreciate that."

"You're welcome," Dunn said. "See you soon." He ended the call.

Chris walked over to his partner. "You okay, J?" he asked.

Jordan smiled. "I am now."

CHAPTER 43

THE JET TOUCHED DOWN at Joint Forces Training Base Los Alamitos. Jordan and Chris exited the aircraft behind Hallier and watched as Commander Egan, hands and feet shackled, was assisted out of the plane by the DARPA soldiers and led to a waiting prisoner transfer vehicle. Armed guards maintained over watch, keeping their weapons trained on him, even for the short walk to the armored car. During the flight they had given the commander a bright orange jumpsuit to wear and assigned three soldiers as his primary escorts. Each man wore a special device on his wrist. The detail maintained a six-foot perimeter around him.

"That's a flashy little number he's wearing," Chris said to Jordan. "What is it?"

"It's called a lightning suit," Jordan said. "If the commander tries to fight or displays any sign of aggression, they'll activate it."

"What happens then?"

"He'll be hit with up to one billion volts of electricity," Jordan explained, "the same amount of energy generated by a lightning strike. Depending upon how high they've set the device it could either stun him, send him into cardiac arrest, or kill him."

"Jesus," Chris replied. "It's basically a wearable

electric chair."

"That's a good way to describe it."

"What do you think is going to happen to him now?"

Jordan shook her head. "Considering the charges he's facing, God only knows."

Hallier waited until the commander's transfer had been completed and the doors to the vehicle were closed and locked. He watched the armored car leave then walked back to speak with the agents.

"I guess that's that," Hallier said. "The commander's back in custody. I don't mind telling you how good that feels."

"Where are they taking him?" Jordan asked.

"Fort Leavenworth, Kansas," Hallier answered. "United States Disciplinary Barracks, Special Housing Unit."

"Will he have a trial?" Chris asked.

"Yes," Hallier said. "Not that it will make much of a difference. He's done."

"How's that?" Jordan asked.

"Commander Egan will be placed on death row."

"How long before he's put to death?" Chris asked.

"Four years," Hallier said. "Maybe less."

"By what means?"

"Lethal injection."

Jordan shook her head. "That's a little ironic, isn't it, Colonel?" she said.

"What do you mean?" Hallier asked.

"First, you injected something into his body that made him the penultimate military asset; a super-soldier, capable of doing anything you asked of him. Soon you're going to inject him again, only this time you're going to kill him."

Hallier wasn't having any part of the conversation. His abrupt attitude returned. He held out his hand. "Your government thanks you for your assistance," he said briskly.

Jordan and Chris shook the colonel's hand.

"One last question, Colonel," Jordan said.

"Yes?"

"Will Commander Egan be allowed visitors?" Jordan asked.

"With special permission, yes."

"I'd appreciate it if you'd be kind enough to let me see him."

Hallier nodded. "That shouldn't be a problem."

"Thank you," Jordan said.

Hallier's car arrived. His driver pulled up beside them, stepped out of the vehicle, opened the colonel's door, saluted, waited. Hallier acknowledged the young soldier.

To Jordan and Chris, he said, "Thank you once again, agents. I'll be sure to let Assistant Director Ridgeway know how helpful you were."

The colonel took his leave.

Chris watched the car drive away. "Pretentious asshole," he said.

"And then some," Jordan replied.

An unmarked FBI sedan approached the jet from across the tarmac, slowed, then stopped. The rear passenger doors flew open. Aiden and Emma jumped out of the car and ran to their mother. "Mom!" they yelled.

Jordan fell to her knees. "Babies!" she cried as the children ran into her arms.

Aiden and Emma hugged her tight.

Andrew Dunn and Marissa stepped out of the car.

"Welcome home, agents," Dunn said.

"Thank you, sir," Jordan said.

"Good to be home, sir," Chris replied.

The children grabbed hold of Chris, wrapped their arms around his waist, hugged him. "I missed you," Aiden asked.

"I missed you too, buddy," Chris said. "Very much."

"I missed you more," Emma said.

Chris held the little girl tight. "Thanks, sweetie pie."

"Hey, Chris!" Aiden said. "Guess what?" The boy was bursting with excitement.

"What, buddy?"

"You should have seen it!" Aiden said.

"Seen what?"

"It was the absolute coolest thing ever! There was this guy, and all of a sudden…"

Jordan quickly interrupted. "Aiden!"

Aiden caught the stern look on his mother's face. "Oops," he said. "Sorry, Mom. I forgot."

"Forgot what?" Chris asked.

"Nothing," Aiden said. "It's no big deal."

Jordan smiled at her son.

Aiden quickly changed the subject. "You're staying

for dinner, right?"

Chris laughed. "That'll be up to your mom." He leaned over, whispered in the boy's ear. "But tell her I'm *really* hungry."

"Can he stay, Mom?" Aiden asked.

"Sure," Jordan said.

"Director Dunn too?"

"Of course."

"Cool!" the children said.

Marissa remained at the car, unsure whether she should approach the family. She held her hand over her mouth. Jordan could tell she was crying.

"Kids," she said. "Can you give Marissa and I a moment alone?"

"Sure thing, Mom," Aiden said.

Jordan walked to her friend.

"I'm so sorry, Jordan," Marissa said. Tears were streaming down her face. "This was all my fault."

Jordan shook her head. "None of this was your fault, Marissa."

"I should have done more to protect the children."

"I know you did everything you could have."

"I'll understand if you want me to leave."

Jordan wrapped her arms around her friend. "That would be absolutely the last thing I would want," she said. She took the woman's face in her hands. "You're my family, Marissa. You're exactly where you need to be. With us. Forever." She dried her tears. "I love you," she said.

Marissa smiled. "I love you too."

Jordan glanced over at the children. "Think you can help me wrangle the kids away from Chris?" she asked.

Marissa laughed. "That's a big ask, but I can try."

"Good," Jordan said. "Let's go home."

∞ ∞ ∞

Woof! Lucy greeted her family and their guests on their arrival at the mansion.

Chris bent down, patted the Golden Retriever. "Hey, girl. Where's your ball?" he said.

Lucy chuffed playfully, then took off running in search of her favorite play toy.

Marissa excused herself. "I'll make dinner. It shouldn't take long."

Jordan put her arm around her. "Not tonight, Marissa," Jordan said. "Tonight, I want you to relax. We'll order in."

"Are you sure?" Marissa asked.

Jordan called out. "Hey, guys. Pizza or Chinese? My treat."

Pizza beat out Chinese by a margin of five to one. It would have been six to one if they had given Lucy a vote.

Chris sat on the living room floor playing with Lucy and the children. Marissa enjoyed a glass of wine.

Director Dunn whispered to Jordan. "May I speak with you for a moment?"

"Of course," Jordan said. She pointed down the hall. "Let's go to the study."

∞ ∞ ∞

Jordan closed the door behind them. "Is everything all right, sir?" she asked.

Dunn nodded. "Just fine. I wanted to bring you up to speed on your case. There are a few details you should know about."

"Did Mannafort harm my children?" Jordan quickly asked.

"Not that we're aware of," Dunn answered. "According to HRT, the children seemed very much in control of the situation. That being said, we're both aware of the effects of post-traumatic stress. I'd recommend they receive psychological counseling just the same."

"I agree," Jordan said.

"Which brings me to Marissa."

"What do you mean?"

"She's been through a hell of a lot, Jordan. Hospital reports confirmed Mannafort used a high-powered stun stick to subdue her. According to the witness who came to her aid, a retired nurse, she was in the throes of a full-blown breakdown when she realized the children were gone."

"I can't even imagine what she went through," Jordan said.

"There's one more thing."

"Oh?"

"We believe Mannafort killed two operatives from

your shadow security team, Holtzman and Bennett. We found their car two blocks from where he'd stopped Marissa and abducted the children. Their credentials were on his body."

"My God."

Dunn continued. "HRT also ran the vehicle identification number of the police sedan found at Mannafort's cabin where the children had been held. It came back to a fellow by the name of Preston Meeks. Meeks was an avid collector of used police vehicles. We found several of them in a barn on his property. He'd posted an online ad for the car found in Mannafort's possession. Mannafort responded to the ad, killed Meeks, then stole the car. We found his body in the trunk of one of his cars. We also found a rental vehicle in the barn which had been reported missing."

"That's where Mannafort had switched cars," Jordan said.

"Correct."

"Bastard."

Dunn nodded. "By the way, after HRT rescued the kids, Aiden told Commander Gibson that Mannafort had confessed to burying ten bodies in the woods outside the cabin. We had a cadaver dog search the area."

"And?"

"It hit on ten locations, exactly as Aiden had said. We're processing the scene now."

"If they've already found ten…"

"There could be more."

"There's a cold case that goes way back," Jordan

recalled. "We studied it at Quantico."

"I know the one," Dunn said. "Fifteen women, all abducted from the San Bernardino, Redlands, Riverside and Moreno Valley areas over the last ten years, presumed dead."

"All of those locations are at the foot of the San Gabriel Mountains."

Dunn nodded. "We may have just found their killer."

∞ ∞ ∞

The pizza was good, the company even better.

After an hour Dunn took his leave, stating his respect for the family's privacy. He ordered Jordan and Chris to take a few days off. The agents gratefully accepted.

"Can we go to Disneyland?" Emma pleaded.

"That would be cool!" Aiden agreed.

Jordan laughed. "All right. If that's what you guys want to do, then that's exactly what we'll do."

"Can Marissa and Chris come too?" Aiden asked.

Chris smiled at Jordan, pointed to the children. "How can you possibly say no to those faces?" he teased.

"Sure," Jordan said. "We'll make it a family day."

"Yay!" the kid's yelled. They ran off to play with Lucy hot on their heels.

Chris walked over to Jordan, put his arm around her. "Family day, huh?"

Jordan smiled. "I did say that, didn't I?"

He smoothed a hair away from her cheek. "Yes, you did."

"I guess it just kind of slipped out."

Chris leaned in, kissed her forehead. "Guess so."

Jordan nestled her head into his shoulder.

"Everything's going to be okay now, Jordan," he said.

"I know."

"We're going to be all right."

Jordan looked up. She smiled. "We're going to be great."

CHAPTER 44

TWO WEEKS LATER

Fort Leavenworth, Kansas
United States Disciplinary Barracks
Special Housing Unit

Jordan sat at a steel table in the visitor's area. Moments later, Commander Egan was escorted into the room.

"Well, this is a pleasant surprise," Egan said.

Jordan smiled. "How are you, Commander?" she asked.

Egan shrugged. "Not bad, all things considered. I'm acclimating."

"How are they treating you?"

Egan smiled. "The roast beef's a little dry and the veggies could use a little spicing up. But on the plus side I'm crushing it on the softball field. I'm thinking now I should have skipped the military altogether, maybe played for the Dodgers. I'm pretty sure they don't kill their players after they retire."

"I'm sorry you had to end up here."

"Me too. It wasn't exactly on my bucket list. On a brighter note, how are your kids?"

"They're doing fine," Jordan said. She removed two

photos from her jacket pocket and placed then on the table. "That's Aiden on the left, Emma on the right."

"They look happy."

"They are."

Egan leaned back. "So, to what do I owe the pleasure?"

"I just wanted to check in, make sure you were okay."

"That was very thoughtful of you."

"Do you think there's any chance they'll commute your sentence?"

"You mean give me life instead of the death penalty?"

"Yes."

"I doubt it."

Jordan shook her head. "This isn't right. You were just following orders."

"Apparently Colonel Hallier doesn't see it that way."

"Hallier's a politician and a puppet."

"Maybe," Egan said, "but this decision came down from Heaven. I'm an embarrassment to the top brass, a reminder they failed. For them, the sooner I'm off the planet the better. Eventually the dust will settle, and when it does all this will be forgotten. DARPA will move on to the next project, maybe even the next Ben Egan."

"It wasn't all for nothing, you know."

"That's true," Egan agreed. "Hernando and the children at Casa de los Niños are safe now. A church in San Jose had offered to take them in. Hopefully, they've made it there."

"Hernando seems like a good man."

"He is. Men like him deserve to receive nothing but good things from this life."

"I can check in on him from time to time if you'd like, let you know how they're doing."

"I would appreciate that very much."

"It would be my pleasure." Jordan checked her watch. "I'm sorry I can't stay longer, Commander. I have to head back to the Bureau."

"I'm glad you came," Egan said.

Jordan picked up her children's pictures from the table, returned them to her pocket, took Egan's hand in hers, stared at him. Egan felt something press into his palm.

"I can't thank you enough for saving my children's lives, Commander," Jordan said. "I only hope that one day you can get out of this place."

Egan smiled. "That would be nice, but it will never happen. The antidote they gave me saw to that."

"Don't be so sure," Jordan said. "Sometimes antidotes aren't as effective as anticipated."

Jordan let go. Egan raised his hand, covered his mouth, coughed, then dropped the object into the chest pocket of his jumpsuit.

Jordan stood. "Be well, Commander."

"You too, Agent Quest."

Jordan walked out the door.

The guard stepped into the room. "That's it, Egan," he said. "No more visitors today. Back to your cell."

Egan stood. "Yes, sir," he replied.

∞ ∞ ∞

Egan waited for the cell door to close. The sound of the guard's footsteps faded as he walked down the hall.

Seated on the thin mattress of the poured concrete bed, he removed the item Jordan had placed in his hand. It was a plastic needle sheath. He examined it closely. Within the protective cover a small drop of pink liquid glimmered. Egan recognized the solution.

He chewed on the end of the plastic sheath, broke it open, felt the metallic taste of the solution on his tongue, swallowed it. His body responded within seconds. He concentrated, felt the vibration in his hand and watched his palm glow, rose red.

He threw the spent needle cover into the toilet, flushed it down the drain, and stared out his four-inch wide cell window which overlooked the courtyard.

The sun was out. The sky was clear and bright. It promised to be a beautiful day.

The only decision that remained was where to spend it.

CHAPTER 45

THREE WEEKS LATER

Sarasota, Florida
Moore Residence

Billy Reynolds skidded his bike to a stop and watched the military sedan park outside his best friend's house. The driver, a young soldier, stepped out of the car, opened the back door and saluted.

The officer exited the vehicle, returned the gesture, walked up the driveway and knocked on the front door. In his hand he carried a black metal briefcase.

James Moore opened the door. "Colonel Hallier," he said. He invited him inside. "Nice to see you under better circumstances."

Hallier smiled. "I agree, Mr. Moore," he replied. "May I speak with Tommy?"

"Of course," James replied. "I'll get him for you."

Waiting in the front entrance, Hallier admired the tastefully decorated home. His last visit to the Moore's had been anything but cordial. A full-on tactical breach had seen to that.

"Hi, Colonel," Tommy said as he walked down the hall.

Hallier shook his hand. "How are you, son?"

"I'm well, sir."

Hallier held up the briefcase. "I have something for you," he said. "Is there somewhere we can we talk privately?"

Tommy motioned to the living room on their left. "Will this be okay?"

"Sure," Hallier replied.

The Colonel and the boy took a seat. Hallier placed the briefcase on a coffee table between them. "This is for you," he said. "First, I'll need your thumb."

"Sir?"

Hallier explained. "This briefcase will be registered to you. After I set it up, the only way to unlock it is by placing your thumb here." He pointed to a small biometric reader located beside the lock.

"Very cool," Tommy said. "Does the case do anything else? Shoot bullets, maybe?"

Hallier smiled. "Not quite. Thumb please."

Tommy placed his thumb on the reader. The indicator light switched from red to green.

"It's calibrated," Hallier said. He opened the briefcase and removed a notebook computer. "This is for you."

"Wow," Tommy said. "Awesome!"

"This isn't a toy, Tommy," Hallier said. "This computer is the property of DARPA. It requires two levels of authentication before it will operate. I'll need your thumb again."

Hallier set up the PC to read Tommy's unique biometric signature then presented him with his login identification. "Read this code and commit it to memory."

Tommy read the unique alpha-numeric password.

"Got it?" Hallier said.

Tommy nodded. "Yes, sir."

"Good." He placed the code in his shirt pocket. "That's it. You're good to go."

"What do you want me to do first, sir?" Tommy asked.

Hallier shook his head. "Nothing. I'll call you when I need you."

"What about those projects?" Tommy asked.

"Projects?"

"The ones I downloaded to the USB drive. Channeler and LEEDA."

"You're not to mention a word of those to anyone. Do you understand?"

"Yes, sir."

"Let me be clear," Hallier said sternly. "Going forward, you'll be using your computer skills to help your government address some of the most sensitive matters related to national security. It's imperative that you fully understand the importance of that responsibility."

"I do, sir," Tommy replied. "I appreciate the trust you've placed in me."

Hallier smiled. "You're a brilliant kid, Tommy. I'm pleased to have you onboard."

"Thank you, sir."

Hallier checked his watch. "I have to leave." He

stood. "Like I said, you'll hear from me when I need you." He held out his hand. "Goodbye, Tommy."

The boy shook it. "Goodbye, sir."

Tommy opened the door, saw the Colonel out.

Billy Reynolds dropped his bicycle on the front lawn. He passed the colonel on the walkway. "How's it going," he said.

Hallier tipped his hat. "Son," he replied.

Billy walked up to Tommy. "Who was that?"

Tommy smiled. "Can't tell ya."

"Why the hell not?" Billy asked.

"Just can't."

"I bet I know."

"Bet you don't."

"I heard about what happened."

"What?"

"The commando's breaching your house, hauling you and your parent's asses out of here. The whole street's talking about it."

"The street doesn't know jack shit."

"Oh yeah? So fill me in. What's the scoop?"

"You want to know the truth?"

"Duh, I'm your best friend. Of course, I want to know the truth."

"It's like I told you before," Tommy said.

"Told me what?"

Tommy waved as Hallier drove away.

He turned to his friend and smiled. "I'm a frickin' genius."

FREE PREVIEW, "LIVE TO TELL"

Please enjoy this free preview of the next book in the Jordan Quest series, "LIVE TO TELL."

CHAPTER 1

THE CUMBERLAND WAS BEAUTIFULLY maintained. Among its luxurious appointments, the bronze Roman urn planters which flanked its main entrance doors overflowed with white evening primrose and purple nightshade. The sweet fragrance of the flowers greeted residents and guests and added to the street level appeal of the tony property. For as long as anyone could remember there had not been a vacancy in the much-desired Westwood Village apartment building. This morning, the white Los Angeles County Coroner's van parked out front alluded to the possibility that one of the much sought after suites might now be available.

A mans voice called out to FBI Special Agents Jordan Quest and Chris Hanover as they walked through the lobby doors. "You guys have to be FBI."

Jordan acknowledged the tall burly figure in the impeccably tailored blue suit as he walked towards her, caught a glimpse of the silver and gold badge clipped to his belt. She smiled. "It's that obvious?"

"You kidding me?" the officer said. "Somewhere there's a Bureau recruiting poster with your pictures on it." He opened his arms. "How are you, Jordan?" he asked.

Jordan laughed, hugged the man, turned to Chris. "Agent Hanover, I'd like you to meet an old friend of my father, Detective James Kerr, LAPD."

Chris smiled, shook the man's hand. "Pleased to meet you."

"Likewise," Kerr replied. To Jordan he said, "Sorry to draw you away from the field. I was hoping to ask for a favor."

"Of course," Jordan said. "Name it."

"This is the third such crime scene I've attended in as many weeks," Kerr said. "You mind taking a look, maybe doing your thing?"

"Not at all," Jordan replied. "Lead the way."

Detective Kerr escorted the agents down the hall. He paused when they arrived at the apartment door. "You ready?" he asked.

"For what?" Jordan asked.

"See for yourselves."

Kerr opened the door. The officers stepped inside the small apartment.

"Oh my," Jordan said.

Scrawled across the living room wall were the words, 'OU PALE OU MOURI.'

"I take it that's blood," Chris said.

"Looks like it to me," Kerr replied. "Forensics are on their way. They'll confirm it when they arrive."

"What happened here, Detective?" Chris asked.

"I'm still trying to figure that out," Kerr answered.

Jordan stared at the words. "What does it mean?" she asked.

Kerr shook his head. "Damned if I know."

From the hallway came an unfamiliar voice. "It means, 'you talk, you die.'"

Kerr spun around. An old man stood in the threshold behind them. "What the hell?" he said. "How did you get past my men?" he asked.

"Dem left," the man replied.

Kerr tried to determine if the man's accent was Jamaican or Haitian, couldn't.

"Smart ting, too," he continued. "Dis no longer a place for God-fearing men. Dis now a place of evil. Best you go too. Lock de door, leave it be."

"Sir, this is an active crime scene," Kerr said. "You need to leave, now."

The old man waved his hand, dismissed Kerr. He pointed a crooked finger at Jordan, hobbled into the room. "De woman, she understands," he said. "Don't you, miss?"

Kerr walked ahead, blocked him from approaching Jordan, took him by the arm. "Did it sound like I was asking?"

"It's all right, Detective," Jordan said. "Let him stay."

"You sure, Jordan?" Kerr asked.

"It's fine."

The detective released the man's arm. Jordan walked over, introduced herself. "My name is Special Agent Jordan Quest. I'm with the FBI. And you are?"

The old man leaned on his wooden walking stick, shook her hand. "Adras," he replied. "Samuel Adras."

"What do you mean by evil, Mr. Adras?" Jordan asked.

"A boko."

"A what?"

"A black priest."

"Are you saying a *priest* did this?"

Adras avoided making eye contact with the death message on the wall, nodded slowly.

"How do you know that?" Chris asked. "Did you see this priest?"

Adras shook his head. "Know de smell."

Chris inhaled, recognized the burnt aroma in the air. "All I smell is incense," he said.

"Not just any incense," Adras replied. "Holy incense."

Kerr looked at Jordan. "I told you this was creepy," he said.

"What's holy about it, Mr. Adras?" Jordan asked.

"De combination," the old man answered. "Musk and cinnamon."

"Is that significant?"

Adras nodded. "De man was creating a barrier between dis world and de next; musk to protect against de power of de boko, cinnamon to boost its strength."

"Are you trying to tell me this guy knew who was trying to kill him?" Kerr asked.

"Yes," Adras answered. "He was trying to keep de evil away, but it was too powerful."

The decedent had been bagged, the body placed on a gurney. "You checked de corpse?" Adras asked.

Kerr nodded. "He had nothing on him."

"You sure?" Adras asked.

Kerr shot the man a defensive glance. "Of course."

"Let me see," Adras said.

"Excuse me?"

"I want to see de body."

"I don't think so," Kerr replied.

The old man stared at the detective. "You afraid I'm going to find something you missed?"

"Now look here," Kerr objected.

"Let him look, Jim," Jordan said. "I want to hear what he has to say."

Kerr partially unzipped the heavy plastic bag. "He's a little ripe," he warned. "You might want to cover your—"

Adras moved the detective aside, pulled the zipper all the way down, parted the bag, inspected the corpse, leaned forward, sniffed. "Dat's it," he said.

"What's it?" Kerr asked.

"De smell."

"Say what?"

The old man grabbed the detective's lapel, pulled him closer to the corpse. "Smell."

Kerr leaned forward, sniffed the body, then suddenly

looked up, stared at Jordan and Chris. "Weird," he said.

"What?" Chris asked.

"He smells like lavender."

"You serious?"

"Check it out for yourself," Kerr said.

Chris sniffed the corpse. "You're right."

"Not just lavender," Adras said. "Patchouli and mugwort. Hyssop too."

"What does it mean?" Jordan asked.

"It's a protection oil," the old man replied. "Keeps you safe from attack."

"From whom?" Kerr asked.

Andras shook his head. "Not from whom, from *what*."

"What are you talking about?"

"Black magic."

"Excuse me?" Chris said.

"Voodoo."

"I told you this was nuts," Kerr said.

The old man patted down the body, pressed on the dead man's pant pocket, slipped his hand inside, pulled out a small satchel.

"What is it?" Kerr asked.

"A conjure bag," Adras replied. He opened the cloth pouch, shook out its contents. A small stone fell into his hand.

"Turquoise," Jordan said. "Why would he be carrying this?"

"To drive de demonic away," Adras said. "Dis man was very afraid." He placed the stone in the bag, returned it to the corpse, then walked over to the window and inspected the sill. "Look, here."

The officers joined the old man at the window. A fine powder had been sprinkled down the length of its frame.

"What is it?" Jordan asked.

"Bloodroot," Adras said.

"What's it for?"

"To keep de evil out."

"That didn't work out so well," Chris said.

Adras ignored the comment. "Did you look in de closets?"

"Of course," Kerr said.

"What did you find?"

"Nothing out of the ordinary."

"You didn't look hard enough," the old man replied. He walked down the hall, opened the linen closet. Neatly folded towels and bedsheets were stacked in the storage space. Adras poked the bottom shelf with his walking stick. "Lift dem out," he said.

Chris kneeled, removed the linens, set them on the floor.

"Take out de shelf," Adras instructed.

Chris pulled up the wooden board, set it aside, exposed the false bottom. "Damn," he said.

A small alter, hidden from view, stood on the closet floor. Chris removed a number of items from the small space: a black candle, a vial of oil, a glass mason jar. The jar contained a photograph.

"Can I see that?" Kerr asked.

Chris handed the detective the jar. Kerr unscrewed

the lid, removed the picture. It was of a young woman. "Couldn't be," he said.

"What is it, Jim?" Jordan asked.

Kerr pulled out his cellphone, accessed the FBI website, opened the Most Wanted tab and began scrolling through the pictures.

"Who are you looking for?" Jordan asked.

"Some people collect baseball cards," Kerr replied. "I follow missing persons reports. I know I've seen this face before." He stopped at one of the pictures, turned his phone towards the agents. "Bethany Rohmer. Last seen eight years ago in New Orleans while attending Mardi Gras with her husband. Disappeared in the crowd. No one's seen her since."

Jordan turned to Samuel Adras. "Do you know why this woman's picture would be in this jar?" she asked.

"He's keeping her trapped," the old man replied.

"Who's keeping her trapped?"

"De black priest. De voodoo man."

Watch for "LIVE TO TELL" coming coon to Amazon.

A SPECIAL THANK YOU TO MY READERS

I'm very fortunate to have many dedicated fans who reach out to me on a regular basis through email and the Jordan Quest Facebook Fan Group. The question I love getting asked the most is, "When is the next Jordan Quest thriller coming out?"

You keep me inspired, pumped and motivated to sit at my desk and punch away at the keyboard with one goal in mind… to make the next Jordan Quest novel a little more suspenseful and fun to read than the last.

I appreciate each and every one of you. You allow me to do what I love the most… to create the stories you enjoy reading.

You guys rock!

Gary

CLAIM YOUR FREE BONUS BOOK

Dear Reader,

Here's what my typical day looks like: wake up at 3 A.M., drink coffee, write stories, drink coffee, write more stories, rinse and repeat. Seven days a week, with the occasional weekend off for good behavior (or if my wife makes me). I do it because I love it.

Building a relationship with my readers is the very best thing about writing. To show my appreciation, I'd like to send you a free ebook, **"JORDAN QUEST, BEHIND THE BADGE,"** right now.

In this exclusive one-on-one interview style book, Jordan answers the questions readers most want to know about both her personal experiences as a world-renowned psychic and FBI Agent and her policing responsibilities with the Federal Bureau of Investigation.

I hope you'll enjoy reading this fun, free book. I'll touch base from time to time with news on the latest Jordan Quest thriller and other cool stuff which I think you'll enjoy. Simply enter the link below into your browser and join my newsletter. Your bonus book will be on its way!

https://www.subscribepage.com/5a1h1

Thanks for reading the Jordan Quest thriller series. It's great having you on board!

Gary

POST A REVIEW

Reviews are the *most powerful* tools in my arsenal when it comes to getting attention for my books.

If you enjoyed reading **NINE LIVES**, I would be very grateful if you could take a minute to post a review on Amazon. It can be as short as you like.

Thanks very much!

Gary

READY FOR MORE?

Each Jordan Quest book can be read as a stand-alone novel.

Listed is the recommended reading order.

THE JORDAN QUEST SERIES

ABOUT GARY WINSTON BROWN

Gary is the author of the popular thriller series, **JORDAN QUEST**. His numerous influences and favorite authors include Dean Koontz, James Patterson, Lee Child, Catherine Coulter, J.D. Robb, Sandra Brown, Kay Hooper and Iris Johansen.

Gary is married and lives outside Toronto, Canada.

Visit the author's website at GaryWinstonBrown.com for more information.

Follow on social media: Facebook   Twitter   Instagram

The Jordan Quest thrillers are best described as tightly written, fast-paced, page-turning suspense mixed with witty-dialogue and high-octane action/adventure. If you like reading stories featuring a tough-as-nails female protagonist (and bad guys you'll love to hate) you're sure to enjoy all the books in the series.

Made in the USA
Middletown, DE
15 August 2020

15387929R00165